I0718418

Spin: Rumpelstiltskin Retold

DEMELZA CARLTON

A tale in the Romance a Medieval Fairy Tale series

This is a work of fiction. Names, characters, businesses, places, events and incidents are either the products of the author's imagination or used in a fictitious manner. Any resemblance to actual persons, living or dead, or actual events is purely coincidental.

Copyright © 2018 Demelza Carlton

Lost Plot Press

ISBN-13: 978-1-925799-25-5

ISBN-10: 1-925799-25-5

DEDICATION

This lucky 13th book in the series is for my awesome readers. Because without you, I would have ended the series at three. So thank you. For reading. And being awesome.

One

Kempenich winced as he reined in his horse. Even that slight movement set off the pain in his chest. Truth be told, he should not be riding at all, and he knew it. But some things could not wait.

The destrier's hooves caught on something, but the horse righted himself before Kempenich was thrown from the saddle. He breathed a sigh of relief. Darkness had carried him into many battles at the order of King

Karl the Great, while the monarch had lived. Now he'd outlived his king, the time had come for what might be his last battle, and he intended to ride the black beast home from this one.

He slid down to the ground. "I seek the witch!" he bellowed. It took every bit of his strength to stand tall and stride toward the cottage, as a knight should.

The witch emerged, her arms folded across her chest. There was pity in her dark eyes, but she stood firm. "I am sorry, Sir Rumpelstiltskin, but there is nothing more I can do for you. You're dying." Mistress Kun turned away.

Sir Kempenich von Rumpelstiltskin refused to admit defeat. "I may be dying, but there is still something you can do for me."

She sighed. "I assure you there is not, but why don't we go inside and discuss it? I can see you need a pain draught. That, at least, I can give you."

Kempenich followed her inside the cottage, then sank gratefully onto a bench. He would drink anything she asked, if only she would grant him one last favour.

Mistress Kun darted about the cottage, assembling what she needed to make the draught, and Kempenich summoned his resolve.

Once more into battle…not for his life, but for the future.

"Mistress, I have heard tales that you are more than a herbwife and healer. More than a usual witch. There are tales that you are what heathens call an enchantress, a woman who works magic. They say that you have power over earth and rocks, and when a child from the village fell down a well, you cracked open the very earth itself to retrieve her, then commanded the rock to return to its previous place, and it obeyed." Kempenich held his breath, praying she would confirm the story.

Kun glanced at him. "There are all sorts of tales. Why, I have heard people tell stories of unicorns and dragons and immortality to children around the fire at night."

Kempenich bowed his head. He, too, had told such tales to his children. Including one he hoped was more fact than fiction. "There is a story about an ancient king who was granted a wish. He wanted to be the richest man in the world, so he wished for everything he touched to turn to gold. It is said that gold comes from the ground, and a wielder of earth magic might be able to do such a thing."

Kun lifted a bucket of water and poured some of it into a small pot over the fire. "Then you must also know the end of the king's tale. He could not eat or drink or touch his family, and he feared his wish would kill him, so he washed his wish away in the river, and shunned gold for the rest of his days."

"I will soon be beyond such mundane things as gold or food or even days, Mistress. But my family will not. And I have spent all that I have in physic for what ails me, seeking a cure that will let me live long enough to restore my family's fortune. If I die now, I will leave them little more than the Rumpelstiltskin house on stilts my father left me, on the rock King Karl granted him for his service. Other knights are building castles along the river to secure their lands, and if my son does not have one, he will lose his lands to a richer man who does. He needs gold, and I would give anything to give it to him."

Kun sank onto a bench and squinted at him in the dim light. "You ask me to curse you. Not for yourself, but for your son, who you will never be able to touch again. You will never be able to eat or drink, and your own wife will not be able to hold your hand as you take your dying breath. You even wish to hasten that dying breath."

"Yes. I am no use to them like this. Better to be dead than to be a burden." Kempenich took the cup she offered and drained it.

Silence stretched between them. But it was Mistress Kun who broke it.

"There is some truth in the tale, but the enchanter who cast such a spell was a fool. I can restrict the spell to your hands, while you live. You may still eat and drink, as long as your hands do not touch it. But when your heart stops, the spell will spread throughout your body, turning it all to gold." Kun bowed her head. "This I will do for you, but you must swear to tell no one about the source of your wealth. Breathe a word to anyone that I cast the spell, and that breath shall be your last."

"I swear on my honour, and that of my father, that I shall tell no one," Kempenich promised.

"Then hold out your hands, palms up," Kun instructed, picking up a knife. She pricked her thumb with the point, then used the welling blood to trace lines on Kempenich's fingers, then his hands, until she swiped her thumb along the lines on Kempenich's wrists, right the way around. "By my blood, I bespell yours. Everything your hands touch from this moment until the day you die, will turn to gold."

For a moment, Kempenich's hands glowed, then lit up in a blinding flash of blue that made him turn his head away, lest the brightness hurt his eyes. When he saw his hands again, the light had vanished, and so had the blood, though the blue tinge to his fingertips had taken on a greenish hue.

Dead hands. Kempenich shivered. Did he dare touch anything with them? What if the spell hadn't worked, and he tainted whatever he touched instead?

"I would offer you a cup of wine to toast your family's fortunes, but…"

Kempenich grimaced. "No more wine for me, now. It does not agree with the draught you gave me."

Kun nodded. "I have just the thing. One of the dairymaids brought a pail of milk this morning, and it's been chilling in the cellar ever since. I mean to keep the cream for butter, but there will be more tomorrow." She rose and headed for the cellar. When she returned, she carried a brimming jug that she poured into two cups and a bowl.

When she caught Kempenich eyeing the bowl with curiosity, she shrugged. "That's for Butter. He usually comes running as soon as I go into the cellar, for he loves his milk." She raised her voice, and called, "Butter! Puss-puss-puss!"

But the cat did not come.

With increasing urgency, the witch kept calling, leaving Kempenich alone in the cottage as she moved outside.

After a while, Kun fell silent. But she didn't come back in.

Kempenich debated whether to follow her, or stay and wait. He wanted to head home before the effects of Kun's draught wore off, but even the walk to where he'd tethered Darkness wore him out these days. He knew in his bones this would be his last ride.

"You did this!" Kun shrieked, bursting into the cottage. In her arms, she cradled a piece of gold-coloured fur.

It took a moment for Kempenich to realise the fur was still attached to a feline body. "I've never seen that cat before," he said weakly. It wasn't a lie. Too late he remembered his horse stumbling as he arrived the cottage. Had Darkness lost his footing because he trod on the cat?

Kun pointed a shaking hand at Darkness. "He had a muddy hoofprint on his back that could only have come from that enormous warhorse of yours. You come here for my help, yet you kill my cat without a care? It's not my fault your ailment is beyond my powers. You, Sir Kempenich von Rumpelstiltskin, have no heart, and that is what is killing you. Take your golden curse, but know this: every male born of your blood will bear the same curse. His heart will fail him in his prime, just as yours has, and his only warning will be the curse, heralding his death. And you – " She waved her hand, and Kempenich found himself soaring through the air, to land in the saddle. "You shall have a daily reminder of the creature you killed." Another wave of her hand, and a pair of gloves appeared on Kempenich's hands.

Golden brown leather, lined with golden fur. Kempenich glanced at her, only to find the cat's corpse had vanished. He now wore it on his hands. His belly roiled, but he fought to keep the bile down.

But Kun wasn't finished. "As long as you wear these gloves, you may touch things like a normal man. Take them off, and all you touch turns to gold. A curse on you, and all who follow you!"

"Please. Curse me…kill me, do what you will with me, but don't hurt my son," he begged.

Her eyes were the cold of black ice. "Bring my cat back to life, and I will consider it."

"Please…"

She clapped her hands. "Go!" The tether holding Darkness broke and he galloped off, forcing Kempenich to cling desperately to the reins so that he would not fall off. "And don't return!" she shouted after him.

As his world dissolved into despair, Kempenich knew one thing for certain: he would never return to the witch's cottage. For if he survived the ride home, it would be a miracle indeed.

He remembered little, until something in the horse's slowing gait made him open his eyes. After several blinks, the blue-green blur before him revealed itself to be the corroded bronze lion that protected the bridge to the island where the house of Rumpelstiltskin stood.

Without thinking, he pulled off his glove and patted the lion's head, as he had done every time he returned home safely. This time, his fingers tingled at the touch, and too late he realised what he'd done. The blueish bronze was neither blue nor bronze any more, but bright, shining gold.

He shoved his hand back into the cat-fur

glove, cursing witches and their cats.

His son would die young, and so would his grandsons, because Kempenich had been a thoughtless fool who sought out a witch. He should have left things well enough alone.

But it was too late now.

What had he done? And how would he ever set it right?

As his vision faded and Kempenich slid from his horse to the ground, fighting for air that did not seem to breathe life into him any more, he had one last, fleeting thought. Even if he died before he could restore his family's fortune, at least his son would have a chance to do it. Before this curse killed him, too.

Two

And so the wheel turns. The flax would flower and fade, the ponds would fill and flow, and through it all Molina would spin and spin and spin, for how else could a woman help the prosperity of her flood-ravaged town?

She stared wistfully at the waterwheels, which never stopped as long as the water flowed down from the mountains. If Lord Bachmeier would only listen to her and let more such wheels be built, their town would be prosperous once more. His grandfather had listened to her grandmother, otherwise these wheels would not be here at all, but to hear the current Lord Bachmeier talk, it was as though nothing had changed since his many-times great grandfather had been given this land from King Karl the Great himself.

If half the stories she'd heard of King Karl, or Charlemagne as the current king called him, were true, he'd have built new wheels all over his empire before the year was out, harnessing the flood instead of complaining about it.

At least Lord Bachmeier had agreed to plant flax in the flood-ravaged fields as soon as the water went down. Which meant an ocean of blue flowers instead of other crops, but they could trade linen for food. Heavens knew precious little grain had passed through the mill this year, but that was just as well, for they needed the spare waterwheels to power the hammers to beat the flax. That had been her mother's design, but Molina had improved on it since. What Lord Bachmeier didn't know wouldn't hurt him.

Molina sighed. She could speed up some of the process, but spinning the flax still took the most time. If she could use a wheel to turn the spindle, this would be so much faster.

"Good day, Miss Molina," a male voice said.

She glanced up in time to see Hofer slap Lanik before Lanik remembered to snatch his cap off his head. "Good day, boys. How goes the spring planting?"

"Almost done, miss. But it looks like the flax on the northern slopes is almost ready to harvest, maybe as early as next week, so we might have to bring the flax up to the pools to soak, and my father sent us to make sure there is water enough up there in the millponds," Hofer said.

"The pools are full, with enough water coming down the mountain to keep the wheels turning," Molina replied.

Lanik coughed. "Beg pardon, miss, but Uncle wanted us to speak to Mister Rademaker."

Of course he did. None of the men in town would take the word of a mere woman over the miller, even if she was his daughter. Molina forced a smile. "Father is beekeeping today. He had his eye on some wild hives further up the mountain, and he thinks they will swarm soon.

He means to capture some new queens for our hives." Their hives were the only ones that had survived the flooding, so if Father didn't capture new bees, there would be no mead brewed in the town at all this year. "I'm sure he'd appreciate the help of two big, strong lads. Maybe even look the other way if a boy managed to get his hands on a honeycomb of his own."

"Yes, miss!"

"Thank you, miss!"

The boys scampered off, too eager at the thought of the possible sweet treat awaiting them to even say farewell. Boys, indeed. They were the same age as she was, old enough to marry, but she'd never see them as anything but the boys she'd grown up with. Certainly not potential husbands, though the other girls in the village didn't seem to share her opinions. Most of them were married already. At this rate, she wouldn't marry anyone, and today would be the same as every day for the rest of her life. She would sit and spin and watch the waterwheels, waiting for her father to return home for the evening meal, wishing for something different.

Today she could do something different. She'd done enough spinning for one day, and the warm breeze whispered of the summer waiting just over the horizon. Perhaps she should go check on the pools herself, and have a swim while she was up there. If the pools would be full of flax next week, this might be her only chance.

She set her spinning inside and dug out a cloth she could use to dry herself afterwards. Flinging it over her shoulder, she set off up the mountain, following the stream to the source of all its bubbling secrets.

Three

Lubos had changed his mind, he decided. Marriage was indeed the happiest state in the world, for if he were at home with his chosen wife, he would not be here in this predicament.

He almost wished he'd simply closed his eyes and agreed to the first girl his father thrust toward him as a possible bride. Instead, he had to endure the company of what felt like hundreds of girls exactly the same as the first. Oh, they might look different, with blonde hair or brown, or even a redhead or two, but whatever colour their eyes had been, he had not noticed. For every girl's eyes held the same look: wide and on the verge of tears. For each girl had been little more than the object of their father's ambition. He wanted her to marry the prince, therefore she was dangled in front of a prince, and it was her duty to ensnare said prince, or forever dishonour her whole family. He did not want to be a duty. He wanted a wife who wanted him, not merely a crown. Yet it seemed once women knew he was the crown prince, the crown part was all they saw.

Lubos had had his fill of such girls at court, which was why he'd happily agreed to his father's suggestion that he accompany the tithe collectors on their rounds this year. Father had told him he suspected a conspiracy among his lords and barons, who were cheating him of his rightful percentage. Lubos, however, smelled a different plot. The recent floods had affected them all, and all of his father's kingdom was poorer because of it. If the tithe was smaller this year, it was because the lords and barons had less to give. Well, to the king, perhaps. Every man among them with a daughter old enough to be out of swaddling clothes wanted to push the poor girl toward the prince, and it was worse than court. Lord Bachmeier was by no means the worst of them, but Lubos had to give him credit for being the most persistent. His four daughters were all old enough to be married, and it seemed the girls had a competition among themselves to see who could win the prince. Lord Bachmeier had boasted about the quality and quantity of linen his lands produced, and it seemed that every lady in the land was employed in making the stuff. His own daughters went everywhere with a spindle in one hand and a distaff in the other, linked by a length of thread. This thread they then used to ensnare him in any way they could.

Why, only last night Lubos had woken from a terrible nightmare. The four girls had turned into spiders, venom dripping from their fangs, as they spun webs to entrap him the moment he moved.

Unable to bear the feeling of fine wool or linen, for it reminded him of his nightmare, in the morning he dressed in his coarsest clothes. But he'd almost screamed when Lorelei let her hair trail over his hand as she filled his cup.

To escape her wide eyes and even wider mouth, for Lorelei had evidently never heard a man utter such an unmanly squeak before, he'd made his excuses and bolted.

He headed to the town at first, a place where the girls did not go, for they believed it was beneath them, or at least their father did. But as he descended into the valley, Lubos noticed a stream with a well worn path beside it that led up the mountain and into the forest. There might be good hunting up here, he thought, which would give him a good excuse to flee from Lord Bachmeier and his daughters in the future, if he needed it.

As he climbed, Lubos heard a strange creaking sound. Like a sign blown in the wind, but it was not a back-and-forth sound. It was as though the wind had picked up the sign and carried it forward, protesting all the way, as it moved ever onward.

Lubos laughed aloud at the thought. Why, the sign was him – moving ever onward from vassal to vassal, protesting when presented with a possible bride at each new castle.

Lubos emerged from the shelter of the trees, and saw the truth. The creaking was driven by water, not wind. Nor did the wood move onward. The giant waterwheels, spinning on their axles in the stream's turbulent flow, could go nowhere. They were anchored in this place as marriage would make him a fixture in his father's castle, for the rest of his life.

A small bridge arced over the millstream, leading to a building as big as any manor house Lubos had visited on his travels. This belonged to the miller, or at least it did now. Perhaps Lord Bachmeier's family had once lived here, before moving to their current castle. He considered crossing the bridge so that he might take a closer look at the house, and perhaps obtain a cup of ale, for climbing this path had been thirsty work. But if this house belonged to Lord Bachmeier still, then any of his daughters might be lying in wait for him there, or one of his servants who might send a runner to find the girls. Either way, his solitary walk would be over.

Instead, Lubos dropped to his knees beside the stream, cupped his hands, and drank. It was cold and sweet, tasting of the mountains it had descended from. Better yet, it slaked his thirst enough to make him choose a higher path – the one that led further up the mountain, following the stream. For if the water tasted so good in the lower reaches down here, how much purer would it be in heights? Determined now, he followed the stream to its source.

Four

Molina trekked up to the pools, panting a little as the slope grew steeper. The track led to the topmost pool, the biggest and deepest of the three. The cool, blue water tempted most newcomers into taking a dip, but Molina knew better. The glacier fed stream was ice cold still when it fed the top pool, and the overhanging trees did little to let the sun in to warm the water. The second pool was little better, for it was cut into the cold stone of the mountain itself, which seemed to drink the warmth the water gained from the sun glittering across its surface.

The third pool, however, was an overflow for the other two. When the snowmelt was too much for the top two pools to take, the water trickled down over the rocks into what was now a third pool, but after Midsummer, would be little more than a depression in the ground, where the softest, thickest grass grew.

Now, it was waist deep – perfect. No trees grew around this pool. The rocks left them no place to take root.

Molina clambered down to the bottom pool, before she stripped off, laying her clothes out on the rocks. She was under no illusions that the water would be warm, and she would appreciate her sun warmed clothes when she donned them again.

She stretched her towel out on the biggest, flattest rock, where it would be within easy reach.

From up here, you could see almost clear to the other side of the valley and all the town in between. If anyone approached, she would spot them at least a mile away, as they took the road leading out of town – more than enough time to dry off and dress.

So she plunged into the water, hissing at that first, cold contact, before she grew used to the temperature and began to wash. She used the soap on her body first, lathering and rinsing as she surveyed the valley below. Then, checking that she could still feel her feet, she decided to take advantage of the afternoon sun to wash and dry her hair, too.

Unbinding it took some time, and washing it even longer, for the thick, dark mane was her only vanity, not that anyone noticed. Most of the other girls in the village had hair in varying shades of flax. The darkness that made her different didn't appeal to any of the village boys. Not that she wanted it to, Molina reminded herself. When she was satisfied that her hair was hidden under the thick layer of creamy lather, she lay back, floating on the surface of the water as she rinsed the soap from her hair. She combed her fingers through it again and again, sending bubbles over the lip of the little waterfall which in turn fed the stream that turned her father's waterwheels.

She squinted at the turning wheels, which

looked like toys from this distance. If she could only attach a spindle to the axle of one, and yet keep the distaff close enough…

Molina shook her head and ducked under the water. Under the surface, the world was murky and green, much like the strange ideas that wanted to take shape in her head. Watermills for spinning and weaving. Why, even Lord Bachmeier thought her daft, having such ideas. Perhaps he was right.

No, she was not daft, she told herself firmly, surging out of the water. Her father listened to her, just as he had listened to her mother. Her ideas were new and different, much like Mother's, and the town did not like different. The floods had proved that. The floodwaters might have washed away crops and buildings, but it seemed the swirling waters had taken some people's sanity with it, too. Once things settled down again, perhaps then they would be open to new ideas. Lord Bachmeier could not live forever.

She used her towel to dry herself off as best she could and squeezed the water from her hair. She pulled on a shift to cover her nakedness, then began to comb her hair. When the tangles were gone, she stretched out on the rock where her towel had lay, letting the sun dry her hair, before she braided it back into a style more suitable for a virtuous miller's daughter. Resting her head in her hand, once again she watched the waterwheels turning, the cogs of her mind turning with them.

A spindle, a distaff, and a wheel…all placed together so that she had no need to hold them, leaving her hands free to spin, and spin faster…

She found a fire pit, long since extinguished, where the farmhands heated up their dinner on flax harvest days, and dug out some charcoal. A piece of bark, caught between two rocks on the edge of the pool, sufficed as her canvas, and Molina began to draw the design taking shape in her head.

Five

A rabbit hopped across the path, and Lubos found himself reaching for his bow out of habit. By the time he nocked an arrow to the string, though, the creature had vanished. It was for the best, he mused, for he was not truly on the road between castles at the moment. If he were, the rabbit would be a welcome addition to the evening stewpot, but if he brought it back to Lord Bachmeier's kitchen, it would surely be wasted, for the man kept a fine table already. Just looking at his four plump daughters could have told Lubos that.

There must be something wrong with him that such examples of beautiful womanhood did nothing for his libido. But his father's vassals were determined to get a betrothal out of him, so he returned home with a bride.

Another rabbit hopped past, slower this time. Lubos pulled out his bow and managed to fire before the creature disappeared, but all he hit was grass.

He cursed. Unlucky in love, and unlucky in hunting. He could do little to improve the first, but the second was within his power. Lubos emptied his quiver, setting the arrows point-first into the ground at his feet. He surveyed his surroundings, and settled on a tree fifty yards away to be his target.

Lubos let the first arrow fly, followed by the rest, before going to retrieve them and try again. He hit the tree more times than he missed, but he could improve. He could.

He fired arrow after arrow all afternoon, until his arms ached and his sweat-drenched tunic stuck to him in the unseasonable spring heat.

His desire to find the stream's source redoubled, and he packed away his bow and arrows so that he might take the mountain track higher still.

A trickling waterfall seemed to be the source of the stream's flow, and he stopped to cup his hands beneath it. He brought the water to his lips and drank. But instead of the pure, sweet water he'd tasted in the lower reaches, this had the distinct taint of something like soap.

Lubos spat it out and wiped his mouth. Had he climbed the mountain in search of pure water, only to find a washerwoman at work? Even now, luck eluded him. He would have to climb higher to find what he sought.

The path curved away from the waterfall, and Lubos took it. He rounded a particularly large boulder and found himself in a positively enchanted clearing, where dappled sunlight filtering through the trees glittered on the surface of a deep pool. A pool with no sign of washerwomen or their work.

Lubos edged closer, until he was near enough to cup his hands and drink. The freezing water numbed his hands, but it tasted so fresh he had to drink more. A sound from below drew his attention, and he peered down the slope.

Ah, he'd thought there was only one pool, when there were actually three. The lowest pool had clothes laid out on the rocks to dry, but there was no one in sight. Perhaps the washerwoman would return?

Lubos paused for a moment. Reaching the third pool would require climbing down rocks. He'd do it, and he could see adventurous youngsters doing it, but a weary wife, burdened with a bag of laundry? He hadn't met a woman yet who wanted to make her work harder.

So he climbed down, determined to satisfy his curiosity, even if he had to wait all day for the washerwoman's return. Either the clothing belonged to a remarkable woman indeed, or there was an easier path he couldn't see from up here.

"Where did you come from?" an imperious voice demanded.

Lubos lost his grip and slid down the last few yards. Thankfully, he managed to land mostly on his feet before he whirled to face his interrogator.

For a moment, he didn't even see her, until he looked down. One of the creamy underdresses was…occupied.

The girl sat up and folded her arms across her breasts. A good thing, too, for the fine linen showed more of them than was decent. "How did you get here?" she demanded.

Lubos had to open and close his mouth several times before his voice came out. "From…from the road from the castle. Lord…Lord…" He couldn't for the life of him remember the man's name, and the more he stared at the girl's dark hair, blowing free in the breeze, the less he could think of anything but her.

"You came from Lord Bachmeier's castle? One of his new labourers, I imagine, as you can't even remember his name. Did he send you with a message for the miller? I'll take it, but next time, you should go straight to the house. No one is to touch the millponds without the miller's permission."

Lubos stared at her outstretched hand, trying to work out what she wanted him to place in her palm.

"Did Lord Bachmeier send you?" she repeated.

He fixed his gaze on her gown, stretched out on a rock. It was as fine as those worn by any of Bachmeier's daughters, though she didn't look anything like them. Her hard curves were half the size of their soft ones, and her dark hair and eyes were midnight to the daughters' cloudy morning light. Exotic. Irresistible. Like no woman he'd ever seen before. And wearing nothing but a shift, as if she wanted to tempt him.

"He must have known I would come here. Made sure you were waiting for me. I must say, if you are the woman he had in mind to warm my bed, Lord Bachmeier's hospitality has definitely improved beyond measure," Lubos said, taking a step toward her.

She was nimbler than he expected, leaping to her feet. In three strides, she was close enough to snatch up her gown and use it to cover her shift.

"The only bed I'll warm is my own, and Bachmeier knows that well," she said with a dangerous glint in her eye. "If he sent you to make trouble for me, then he must truly hate you. A man with no honour, who has not even the courtesy to turn his back when he stumbles across a woman in a state of undress…perhaps this is the first time I will share Bachmeier's opinion."

A washerwoman with a fine gown, so close to the manor house by the mill…this was the miller's wife. And he'd just treated her like a common harlot.

Feeling his face grow hot, Lubos bowed low. "Forgive me, Mistress Miller. I was struck dumb by your beauty." He kept his eyes firmly on the ground at his feet.

"Dumb means you cannot talk. You may have a problem with your tongue, but that is not it," she said gently. "You are new here, so I will forgive you this once, farm boy, as long as you do not say such things again."

Farm boy? Lubos almost laughed, then realised she had based her assessment on his clothes. If he told her who he truly was…

Then she would be less forgiving, for a prince should know better.

"Thank you, mistress," he said.

He waited, but received no response. Finally, he lifted his head, only to find the girl had gone. She'd dressed and disappeared. Leaving nothing behind.

Something blew from behind him, and he reached out instinctively to catch it. It was a piece of bark, bleached in the sun until it was as pale as parchment. But it wasn't the bark that held his attention. It was the sketch on it. A few lines, scrawled in charcoal, but he could clearly make out the shape of the waterwheels below, connected to what looked like a spindle and distaff. Her work, it must be…

Tucking the piece of bark inside his tunic, he began to make his way back to Bachmeier's castle. But he saw nothing of the road, no matter how many rabbits hopped across his path. All his vision was occupied by a pair of glittering dark eyes that belonged to the miller's wife.

Six

Her father was jubilant about getting three new queens for the hives, and Helga had made a particularly fine stew with dumplings before heading back to the village for the evening, so Molina did her best to forget the strange encounter with Lord Bachmeier's new farmhand. For a moment there, she'd thought Bachmeier had sent the boy to kidnap her and force her to become his bride.

But Bachmeier wouldn't do such a thing, surely. He'd asked, she'd refused, and he'd insisted she would regret her decision when he chose another. He'd said it dismissively, as though he cared little what she regretted, for he would have shifted his affections elsewhere, if indeed they existed at all,.

"The village boys still fear you. What in heaven's name did you do to scare them so?" Father asked.

Molina considered her response carefully before she said, "Oh, they think I'm a witch, because I know how the waterwheels work." Actually, it was more likely they blamed her for that Easter festival when she and a few of the other people her age had drunk too much wine and decided to celebrate some ancient pagan fertility festival that Rikard insisted was celebrated at the same time. They'd all paired up, taken their clothes off, and proceeded to see how fertile they were. Two of the girls fell pregnant that night, but when Rikard entered Molina, she'd cried out so loudly at the pain that she'd killed his desire, too. He claimed she'd cursed his manhood with her barrenness, and as she was the only girl not carrying a child, the others believed it.

But she had no intention of telling her

father that.

"Bachmeier won't wait forever. A lord like him will lose patience eventually, and decide to take what he wants. You should choose a husband, and marry the man soon. Then Bachmeier will turn his eyes elsewhere."

Molina shrugged. "None of the village men are a better choice than Bachmeier, for if they were, I'd be married already. My passion is for waterwheels and what we can make with them. Machines, not men."

"That's what your mother said, too. Did you know the first time I kissed her, it was behind the mill? And one day when we went swimming in the millpond together…"

"I know, I know, you've already told me," Molina interrupted, not wanting to hear about the first time her parents got naked together. It reminded her too much of the disturbing events of the afternoon. "Does Bachmeier have some new workers up at his farm?"

Father frowned. "Not that I've heard. Plenty of boys here in the village who would jump at the job, for Bachmeier offers married quarters for the men who work for him. Better than sharing a house here in the village with several generations of your family, or so they say." He brightened. "But the king's tithe collectors are on their way. They've been to the other provinces and we're bound to be next. If you have your heart set on a man not from the village, one of the king's men might be your best chance. Especially if he takes you back to the capital. Bachmeier might not listen when we tell him what our waterwheels can do, but I'm sure the king will care."

"I'm not seducing one of the king's soldiers," Molina objected.

"How about one of the king's knights? Or a nobleman from court? The tithe is the most valuable thing in the countryside, and he sends his best knights to protect it. Have you ever seen a man in armour?"

Molina considered for a moment. "No, but I can't see how armour is meant to be attractive. I mean, you cannot see his face under the helmet, and what if you cut yourself on the metal trying to undress him? Marrying a knight sounds like a good way to get hurt."

Father shook his head. "Once again with all

the thinking. Your mind never stops. Your mother would be so proud, but she'd be telling you even louder that village life will never be enough for you."

"It was for her!"

Father smiled sadly. "She stayed for me, and because she got to build the waterwheels the way she wanted them. Without a new project or someone to love, she would never have stayed. The waterwheels are as good as they will get, yet I know you have ideas almost daily. Tell me what you thought of today."

Father knew her too well. Molina relented. "Today I got sick of spinning, so I designed a machine that holds the spindle and the distaff and turns the spindle with a wheel. You could attach it with gears to a waterwheel so it spins at just the right rate…"

Father laughed. "Show me."

Molina felt in her bodice, where she usually stashed her sketches, but found none. "Damn. I must have left it up by the pools. A man came and distracted me, so I came home earlier than I intended. I'll go up there tomorrow to retrieve it so I can show you. I really think this will work. I would have to build it and try it first, but I think this can easily halve the time I spend spinning. It all depends on the speed."

"If Bachmeier agreed to let you try half the things you think up, no one in the village would have to work at all. He's a fool for not listening to you. His only redeeming feature is his good taste in wine. And women, for he did choose you over the other girls in the village." Father poured himself a cup of wine and leaned back on his bench, until his head touched the wall. "If you were younger, I'd tell you one of those fairytales, where a knight in shining armour comes to woo the lovely young miller's daughter, carrying her away on his horse. For all that I wish there were such a man for you, even I doubt it in this day and age. All the modern knights seek fame and glory in tourneys or crusades, not love. Yet I wish it for you with all my heart."

Molina forced herself to smile, for her father's words reminded her of the loneliness that made her heart ache at night. "I have you and your love, Father. I am lucky to have the love of one wonderful man. To have the love of two…seems to be asking too much of fate. Perhaps we should not tempt her so."

Father leaned forward. "Or perhaps that is exactly what we must do. Tempt fate, so that she might change something to make your life more interesting. Maybe not a knight. Maybe a man with rank equal to Bachmeier, who will treat you as you deserve, and listen to your schemes. You know, the ancient goddess of fate here was a spinner. Your new spinning wheel might be just the thing to get her attention. Tomorrow, you must find that sketch, and tell me everything, for we will build it together."

Molina's heart lifted. It had been a long time since her father helped her with a project. "Thank you, Father. That sounds perfect."

Seven

Dinner with Lord Bachmeier and his daughters didn't fill Lubos with dread as it had yesterday. He barely noticed when the girls brushed against him, though he could not deny his relief when Bachmeier sent his pouting daughters to bed.

When Lubos rose to retire, Bachmeier held up his hand. "Please, let me share some of my best vintage with you, Your Highness. Such fine wine is not fit for women, but for the likes of us, who can appreciate such things…"

Lubos wondered whether the miller's wife

liked wine, fine or otherwise. Perhaps he could send her a cask of the stuff on the morrow, to make up for his rudeness today. He suspected it would need to be a very rare vintage indeed to gain her good opinion, if she even liked wine.

"Did you enjoy your day, Your Highness?" Lord Bachmeier asked, pouring the wine into two goblets.

"Yes," Lubos said absently. "I have heard much about the watermills here, and I wanted to see them for myself."

It was a lie, but one that made the other man preen with pride.

"They were built by one of my great uncles, who saw such things on his travels," Lord Bachmeier boasted. "A younger son, so he had no hope of inheriting the castle. He travelled widely and brought home a wife from foreign parts. Eventually, he made a home for himself and his descendants in the old manor house beside what is now the millstream."

Lubos cursed himself. That made the miller's wife the highest woman in Bachmeier's lands, second only to Bachmeier's lady, if she'd still lived. Probably nobly born, judging by her clothes. Trust him to insult her.

He glanced up to find Lord Bachmeier staring at him, as if waiting for a response. "I'm sorry, it has been a long day. Could you repeat that?"

Lord Bachmeier didn't seem to be offended, though perhaps his near-empty wine cup had something to do with that. "I asked if you met the miller. Rademaker is a good man. 'Twas his idea to plant flax when all our autumn sown crops washed away. We have the finest linen anywhere, and now there will be even more of it!"

"No, I did not. I will return on the morrow to see him." And her. Lubos prayed he would not make a fool of himself again. He pulled the bark out of his tunic, and held it out. "Perhaps you can tell me something. Is this contraption the secret of your linen production?"

Lord Bachmeier squinted at the crude drawing, his lip curling in disgust. "Our women will not sit idle while a machine does their work! That girl is delusional to think otherwise. Not a week passes that she does not come up here, nagging me about how her inventions could make this province rich if I only surrendered to one of her insane plans. She'd be better served settling down and birthing children for her husband, like the other women in the village. Rademaker will not live forever, and we cannot be without a miller." He threw the bark down on the table and poured himself another cup of wine. "Drink up, man!"

Lubos took the cup in one hand, reclaiming the bark with the other. As he sipped the wine, his mind whirled. The miller was an old man, with a young wife? As the miller's wife, he had no business thinking of her, but once she was the man's widow…

A less honourable man would help matters along, but Lubos would not stoop to murder, even over a beautiful woman.

A woman who claimed she could create wealth with her wheeled contraptions…

Lubos would return to the mill on the morrow, and ask the girl herself. Perhaps Lord Bachmeier was right and she was not right in the head, but Lubos doubted it. He'd never looked into a more lucid pair of eyes than hers.

"What is the madwoman's name?" Lubos asked casually.

"Molina," Lord Bachmeier muttered. "Bane of my life, Molina. Wouldn't marry me when my wife died, either."

So she'd chosen the miller over being Lady Bachmeier. Lubos really did need to meet the miller. On the morrow, he promised himself.

"To women, though they may drive us mad," Lubos announced, lifting his cup in a toast.

Lord Bachmeier filled and lifted his own. "To good women," he said.

Both men drank, their thoughts on the same woman. But only Lubos wore a smile.

Eight

"I'm going to have a son," Maja said proudly. "I visited Dalia, the witch woman in the woods today. She is a seer, you know, and she is certain the baby will be a boy. You will be a father, Abraham."

Chase clapped Abraham on the back. "Congratulations!"

But Abraham felt no joy in the news. Being born a boy in his family was a death sentence. He knew, for his time had already started to drip away. Without a word, he rose from his seat and left the hall.

The spring air still held winter's chill, as its icy breath swirled around him in the dark. No breeze could ever be as cold or dark as the invisible hand clenched around his heart as he stood on the battlements, and wished he dared throw himself off them into the river below.

But he could not. Death would find him soon enough, and hastening it would not save his son.

"Now you've done it. My sister won't stop sobbing that her husband no longer loves her. First you won't touch her, and now this. What man isn't happy to know he'll have a son and heir?" Chase demanded, emerging out of the dark. "I gave her my word I would call you out if it's true, for it's my duty as your friend and your brother in law to beat some sense into you."

"Do you believe in magic?" Abraham asked.

Chase laughed. "You mean do I believe the witch? Maybe. I do not know. What does it matter? My sister knows she is carrying a baby, and that it is yours, which is good enough for me. You should be celebrating!" He shoved a cup at Abraham, but Abraham didn't take it.

"Suit yourself, then. I shall drink to your good fortune!" Chase drank it down in three gulps.

"I don't mean her. Have you heard the stories about where my family got the lion at the gate?" Abraham pointed at the statue on the bridge below. Even from up here, he could see it shine in the torchlight.

Chase shrugged. "It looks ancient, like it was taken as a trophy when one of your ancestors conquered some city or other. I mean, who would make something so big in bronze any more?"

"It's not bronze. It's solid gold," Abraham said. "When Kempenich the Cursed touched it, he called down a curse on every male in our bloodline. Or so my father told me. I didn't believe him – not even on his deathbed, when he made me swear to find some way to break the curse – but now…"

"Some curse. You have a bigger castle than any lord in the land, and more wealth than you know what to do with. A solid gold statue that guards your gate…why, that sounds like the kind of curse I would beg for, not break!" Chase laughed.

"Give me the cup," Abraham commanded.

"Now you want wine. Good thing I brought a whole jug," Chase said. He refilled his cup, and handed it to his brother in law.

Abraham took the cup, then tugged off one glove with his teeth and wrapped his bare hand around the clay cup. He lifted it to his lips and drank, wishing he could drown his dread. But Chase needed to know, for someone would have to take care of Maja and the baby when he was gone.

When the cup was dry, Abraham threw it down on the flagstones at his feet. Instead of the tinkle of broken ceramic, the cup merely clanged and rolled away.

"What in heaven's name…?" Chase began.

Abraham replaced his glove. "Pick it up. It'll be gold, like the statue, now. Like anything I touch without the gloves."

Chase whistled. "Everything you touch turns to gold? No wonder your family is so rich. Here, do my dagger." He unsheathed the knife and held it out.

"A gold dagger is too soft to be any use. Put it away. It's a curse. My family's curse."

"It does not sound like such a curse to me."

Abraham sighed. "If you could not touch the woman you love without gloves on, you would understand."

Realisation dawned in Chase's eyes. "So that's why…Maja…why didn't you just tell her?"

"Because there's more. The curse only comes when the men of House Rumpelstiltskin are close to death. None of the men in my family have lived for more than a year once they have the Touch."

Chase looked stricken. "How long? Will you live to see the babe born?"

Abraham shook his head. "That's just it. I don't know. I just woke up one morning, reached for the door of the garderobe, and the handle turned cold under my hand. If I'd touched Maja instead…" He shivered. "I haven't taken my gloves off since. My father gave them to me on his deathbed, and told me I would know when to use them. As it turns out, they're the only thing I can touch that doesn't turn to gold. They must be magic, too."

Silence reigned on the battlements, but for the burble of the river, far below.

Chase broke it. "You need to tell her."

Abraham laughed bitterly. "Tell her what? That she married a man whose family is cursed? That I'll never be able to touch her again, for the rest of my short life, and, even worse, our son will suffer the same fate? I didn't believe it, not even when my father told me on his death bed. I was a child, and thought he was telling me some fairytale about a man and a witch and a lion. Not until I saw what I'd done to the garderobe door did I think there was any truth in his tale!" He buried his head in his hands. "If I'd known, I would never have courted Maja. Never married her, never lain with her, for to visit this fate on a child...our child! I deserve my fate. And I do not have enough days to make it up to her. I will die unforgiven."

"My sister loves you, and even if she had known, I'm not sure even I could have stopped her from marrying you. And...I've seen the way you look at her. I know you would never seek to hurt her. You're an honourable man, Abraham. When you vow to do something, you do everything within your power to make sure it happens. You will not die in dishonour. Fulfil the vow you made to your father, and break the curse. For your father, for Maja, for your unborn son…for the future of your family."

Abraham didn't deserve the blind faith in Chase's eyes. And yet…more than anything, he wanted to believe his brother in law's words.

Slowly, Abraham nodded. "Though my time is short, I solemnly vow, with you as my witness, that I shall spend every waking moment I have left, working to break Kempenich's curse, so that my son will be free."

Chase leaned over to retrieve the golden cup Abraham had dropped. "I'll hold you to it, my friend. And I'll keep this as a souvenir. I always did want to drink out of a golden cup."

Abraham reached out to cuff his friend, but drew his hand back. Until he died or broke the curse, he would have to be careful of everyone and everything he touched. Just in case.

For now, more than ever, Abraham believed

in magic. He would visit the witch on the morrow, so that the seer might tell him his future. And he would not leave until she told him a tale with light at the end, not merely gold and death.

Nine

Find the wealth the barons are hiding in the countryside, his father had told him. Find it, and bring it home. The words became a litany in Lubos' head as he headed back to the mill. Bachmeier wasn't so much hiding Molina as keeping her to himself, and squandering her talents besides. If she truly could create things that would make the kingdom wealthy…make women's work go faster…

Just as men looked up to their king, a kingdom's women looked to their queen. They would do their best to fashion clothing like hers, name their children after her, attend royal events just to get a glimpse of her, and maybe receive her blessing. Even his mother, who'd done little more than smile wanly as the constant pregnancies and miscarriages took their toll. Yet a wave from her could make a crowd erupt in louder cheers than those for his father.

He'd heard tales of the legendary Queen Margareta of Aros, who ruled beside her husband as his equal. The stories said men willingly laid down their lives for her, for it was an honour to serve such a lady. It was even said that she was responsible for turning her kingdom into a great sea empire, though that could be because her dowry came with Beacon Isle. But even Lubos had heard of Beacon Isle, an independent island that was the greatest trading port in the northern sea, occupied by people who called no man king. But they answered to Queen Margareta.

If Lubos returned to his father with a wife as formidable as Queen Margareta, a woman who could hold her own against her liege lord and make the kingdom prosper again…

Well, his father would be pleased. He'd finally leave off trying to make Lubos marry some soft, insipid girl, and Lubos would be free to live the life he'd dreamed about. Well, last night he'd dreamed about it, or more specifically, her.

Dreamed of helping Molina out of that thin shift, so he could see her in all her naked glory, before making love to her as a queen deserved.

Please, let the miller be so old and decrepit he was ready to knock on death's door, Lubos prayed as strode up the path to the mill. What had the man's name been? Rademaker. A good man. Lubos prayed the man would soon receive his reward in heaven…

"You must be one of the king's tax collectors, come to inspect the mill. I had begun to think Lord Bachmeier had forgotten to mention it to you."

Lubos looked up to meet the eyes of a man who looked younger than Bachmeier, or even his own father. A man whose fine linen clothes marked him as more than a farmhand.

The man held out his hand. "I'm Rademaker, and I welcome you to our town.

We have a particularly fine watermill, thanks to my very talented wife."

Lubos' heart sank right down into his boots. Rademaker was a man in his prime, perhaps forty years old at most, with only a slight greying at his temples to show he was no longer a young man. Yet Lubos summoned a smile, for it was not Rademaker's fault he was the luckiest man in the world. "I would love to see the watermill. I came yesterday, but…"

"I was not at home. The wild bees were swarming, and I wanted to catch some new queens for our hive. They produce better honey up here on the slopes than in the lowlands of the valley, and Lord Bachmeier is particularly partial to it. Before the floods, he was often willing to trade a flagon of his best imported wine for my honey, but now that my hives were the only ones to survive the floods, I must increase production to meet the demand. And maybe even the price, too." Rademaker winked. "I fancy my honey is never part of the tithe Lord Bachmeier sends to the king, but I will happily make a gift of it for His Majesty. If you promise to make sure the king receives it, I shall give you some for yourself, too."

Lubos mumbled his thanks, forcing a smile at the thought of such sticky sweetness. He was not overly fond of honey, preferring sharp spices to season his food. Nor was he fond of wine, for the alcohol dulled his wits. It did put him in mind of the gift he'd brought, though. "I brought a gift for you, too, Master Rademaker. Lord Bachmeier's best imported wine, I believe." He held out the flagon.

Rademaker laughed. "Ah, I see why the king sent out a clever man like you. You have come to uncover all the lords' secrets. I will share ours freely, for it was my wife's dearest wish to see such watermills all over the country. I hope you will take a good account of us back to the king."

How was Lubos to tell the man it was his wife he wanted to take to the king, not tales of watermills? Lubos forced down his raging jealousy and said, "Show me, and we shall see."

Rademaker ambled up the hill with Lubos, pointing out the pools that fed the millstream, and detailing the output of the mill itself.

Lubos learned that the watermills did not just grind grain. They were used to process the flax that made the region's fine linen. Bachmeier had lied, or he did not know of it. Perhaps Molina had made the modifications to the mill without her lord's knowledge or permission. Lubos wouldn't put it past her.

Lubos looked over the waterwheels, turning swiftly in the current. All but one, that seemed more sluggish than the rest. "What's wrong with that one?" he asked.

Rademaker shrugged. "I don't know. It was fine yesterday, but something must have happened overnight to slow it down. Let's see, shall we?" He led the way up to the slow wheel. "What ails it?" he called.

A dark figure emerged from the other side of the wheel. Lubos' breath caught in his throat. Molina stood thigh deep in the water, her skirt kirtled up so as not to get wet. "There's something stuck in it," she said, peering between the paddles. "I can almost…there!" She dived through the paddles, into the middle of the spinning waterwheel.

"No!" Lubos shouted, leaping into the water to save her. He was soaked in an instant, but he did not care. He wrapped his arms around her waist and dragged her away from the wheel that wanted to crush her. Too late he realised that she wore nothing beneath her skirts, and her pale buttocks pressed against his groin woke up his libido in the most painful way.

Then something slapped him in the face, harder than any woman should be able to, and the girl wrenched out of his grasp.

Stunned, Lubos shook his head, trying to clear it.

"Get out of the water before you freeze to death, you fool!" she ordered. "Go, before I release the wheel and it wets you even more!"

Lubos blinked. She'd somehow stopped the waterwheel. She hadn't been in danger at all. Fool that he was, he'd grabbed her and now the iciest water in the world wouldn't return the blood that flooded his nether regions back to his head so he could think. Think about anything else but cupping that bottom in his hands as he made love to her...

"Suit yourself, then."

Lubos didn't have time to register her words before a wave of water hit him, knocking him on his arse in the stream as the wave washed over his head. He came up spluttering. Near drowning had cooled his ardour somewhat by the time he managed to struggle ashore.

Molina stood beside her father, her skirts let down to cover her lovely legs once more, as she folded her arms across her breasts.

"You'd best come up to the house, Master Lubos. Molina will find you some dry clothes while we dry yours, and it seems only fitting that you stay for dinner."

"We're having trout," Molina said, dropping to her knees on the grass. Lubos got another peek under her skirts as she leaned forward to slash her knife across the fat fish's throat before she rose, lifting the fish by the gills.

The fish had slapped him, not Molina, Lubos realised, touching his cheek.

"Quite a chivalrous creature, even if it is a fish," Molina added, as if reading his mind.

Red-faced, Lubos followed her into the house.

Ten

The witch had hair fluffier than a fresh-shorn fleece. Abraham prayed that her thoughts were not as woolly-headed as she appeared.

"Ah, 'tis the boy's father, come to call. And not to ask about the baby, or the chest pains, though I have prepared a draught for you, all the same." The woman smiled and gestured toward the table outside her cottage, and the steaming cup that sat beside a suspicious-looking, smoke-coloured cat.

Abraham had no intention of drinking some witch's potion. Her talk of chest pains made his ribs ache, though he was certain there had been no pain before.

"I did not curse you. It was another witch, long ago, who cursed your ancestor, but I promise you, the chest pains started when you turned that garderobe handle to gold. You just did not notice until now. And the draught is not poisoned. It will ease the pain so that you no longer notice it, at least for a little while."

"Do you read minds?" he asked.

She laughed softly. "No, Sir Abraham, I do not see into your mind. Instead, I see into the future of what will be, or what it might be. But you do not wish to ask me what will be, for you already know your fate."

His voice came out in a whisper: "Less than a year from now, the curse will consume me completely, and I will die, and my legacy will be to pass the curse on to the very son my wife is carrying, so that in his turn, the curse will consume him, too."

Her eyes were unusually hard in such a soft face, but they arrowed into his soul. "So tell me, Sir Abraham. If you know the future is so certain, why have you come here? What can you possibly want to ask of me?"

It was on the tip of his tongue to say that such a strong seer would surely know the words before they left his lips, but as he gazed into her knowing eyes, the urge left him. To let her speak for him was to let fate have her way with his life, and he would surrender to fate no longer.

"I have come to ask how to change my fate. To break the curse that kills my family, for a crime so far in the past none of us can remember it. A way to save my son, and fulfil the oath I made to my father."

"Save the boy, or save yourself?" she asked sharply.

Abraham did not flinch from her gaze. "Both of us, if I can. But if I can save the boy from sharing my father's fate, it will be enough."

"Would you give your life to do it?"

For a long moment, Abraham could not answer. Finally, he said, "All men die. If I do nothing, my time is already short."

She nodded slowly, as if this answer seemed to satisfy her. "Drink the draught, Sir

Abraham."

He reached for the cup, clenching his gloved hand around it, and downed the contents. Heat seared his throat, bringing tears to his eyes as he coughed and…ah, now his chest hurt. But it was a small pain, too small to mention. He slammed the cup back on the table. "Satisfied?" he growled.

"It is not my good opinion that matters, brave knight, but a girl who you have yet to meet." The witch closed her eyes. "You must go to the capital, and as you cross the bridge into the city, look up. You will see a tower, and there you will find the girl. She will be in danger, though she may not know it yet. You must keep her alive, no matter what happens, in order for her to break the curse. She must break it willingly, of her own free choice, even though she does not know how to do it. She is your only hope, and if she dies, then all hope is lost."

"Does this girl have a name?"

The witch shook her head. "I cannot control the visions, Sir Abraham, nor can I know everything. You have a time and a place to be, and the certainty that she is the right person. I cannot tell you more than I can see."

Despair welled up in his breast, threatening to swallow his heart. "But I must know more. Must I leave now, or can I say farewell to my family? Will she break the curse right away, or will I have to wait? Will she do it in time to save me, or save him? What if...?"

There was pity in her eyes now. "You will leave on the morrow, and you will have time to say farewell to your wife tonight. Once you arrive in the capital, your fate, and that of your son, will be in your hands. When and how and who...are questions I cannot answer, for they depend on what lies in your heart, and what you choose to do. One thing I can promise you. If you choose to stay, and do not travel to the capital, then both you and your son will die, exactly as you have foretold, and you will die an oathbreaker."

"I will not die an oathbreaker!"

She smiled. "Then perhaps your son will live to hold his own son in his arms. Oh, and one more thing. I cannot tell you more, but I can give you a gift that may make your task easier.

They were a gift to me, and heaven knows I have no use for them."

She headed into the cottage, then returned a moment later with a pair of extraordinary shoes. They were made of black leather so dark, they seemed to drink the light. They were not new, for dust scuffed the toes, but they seemed hardly worn at all.

"Keep them," Abraham said, waving her gift away. "I have no need for another man's cast-off shoes. My family's curse has the fortunate result of keeping us wealthy enough to afford good boots."

"Ah, but can your good boots do this?" she asked, slipping the shoes on her own small feet. She stamped her foot three times. A hole appeared at her feet, small at first, then widening, until it was large enough to swallow her. The witch grinned, then stepped forward. She dropped through the hole, which closed abruptly behind her.

Abraham's mouth dropped open and he could not seem to close it. He scuffed his foot across the ground where the hole had opened, but it felt perfectly solid to him, as if the hole had never been.

The witch's breathy laugh came from behind him, and Abraham whirled to find her standing in the doorway to the cottage with her arms folded across her chest.

"My cellar is beneath you, Sir Abraham. Or, more specifically, my bags of flour for baking. I landed on the sacks, and came up the stairs to where I am now. Such is the magic of the shoes. Merely stamp your foot thrice while wearing them, touch your toe to the point where you want the hole to form, and it shall open. It works on walls as well as floors. It will close when you have passed through it, just as you have seen." She held out the shoes. "In all the best tales, a knight on a quest receives a magical item to help him. Make the tale a good one, Sir Abraham. One that will be remembered through all the ages, so that a thousand years from now, when the nights are long and dark, someone will start to tell the tale of the man from House Rumpelstiltskin, and how he saved a princess from a terrible fate."

Abraham bowed. "I thank you for your gifts

and your sound advice, Mistress Witch, and I will do everything within my power to be the hero of such a tale." He mounted his horse, waved farewell, and headed home.

Dalia shook her head and reached out to stroke the cat on the table. "Should I have told him that when his tale is told, there are those who will think he is the villain, and not the hero, Kisa?"

"Mrow," said Kisa, angling her head to give the witch better access to her neck.

Dalia sighed. "Better that he does not know, then. The people of the future must make up their own minds, as he will, when the time comes for him to choose."

Eleven

Lubos stripped off his wet clothes, shivering in front of the fire. As if his dreams from last night weren't bad enough, now he'd have visions of what she really looked like under her dress. Even the memory of her pressed against him had him hard as rock all over again.

There was only one way to deal with this — short of bedding the girl herself, which he knew would never happen. Not now he'd made an idiot of himself twice in front of her.

He found a chamber pot under the dresser, and wrapped his hands around himself. As if in answer to his prayer, he spotted a bark sketch on the dresser, capturing in a few lines the beauty of the woman in his head. Dark hair, dark eyes, the swell of her breasts beneath her gown…

He stroked and stroked, never taking his eyes from her, until finally he groaned, "Oh my God, Molina," as he experienced that glorious release.

A breath huffed out behind him. "I'm not sure whether to be appalled or appreciative. Did you just pleasure yourself in front of my mother's picture?"

Lubos covered himself with his hands, unable to hide his flaming cheeks. Now he truly was struck dumb.

Molina stepped through the doorway, carrying a pile of clothing that she thrust at him. "You're bigger than the boys in the village. Is it because you're better fed as the king's tax collector, or is it a tribute to your desire for my mother?"

"I thought the picture was you," Lubos managed to say, then instantly regretted it.

Her lips twitched in what might have been a

fleeting smile, before her frown returned. "First watching me bathe yesterday, now pleasuring yourself in front of my picture. Most men would call you crazy, Master Lubos. Especially when you're staying at the castle with Lord Bachmeier's four beautiful daughters willing to do almost anything to catch a husband. I'm surprised he let you leave the castle confines, if you are a bachelor."

"I like brunettes," he said weakly.

"So I see," she said. "Is it supposed to rise again so fast?"

Mortified, Lubos moved his hands to cover himself again.

"Get dressed, while I take these outside to dry." She gathered up his wet clothes. "They are much finer than the ones you wore yesterday. You should have corrected me when I called you a farm labourer. Or at the very least introduced yourself."

"I...I was..." He couldn't seem to finish his sentences around her.

"Struck dumb, or so you said. Yes. Get dressed. Though not as fine as your own garments, these things should at least fit. If anyone in the village were to hear I'd been alone with a nude man on a mission from the king, all the old ladies would die of shock."

She swept out of the room.

Lubos slumped. Thrice he'd made a fool of himself. He'd never be able to look her in the eye again. Let alone her husband.

When he'd managed to cover himself up enough to satisfy even the most modest old woman from the village, Lubos crept down the stairs, wondering if he could escape without anyone seeing him. He'd trade his own clothes for these happily if it meant not seeing…

"Ah, good, they fit. I was worried you might be too big for them," Rademaker said. "One of the village boys just told me about another hive swarming, that I hope to catch. Molina can show you around the mill. No one knows the workings of this place better than she does."

He stuck a hat on his head and departed, leaving Lubos to stand with his mouth agape in the dining hall.

"So, are you truly interested in the mill, or are you and my father cooking up some sort of scheme together?" Molina asked, appearing in the doorway.

"I've never met your father," Lubos protested.

Molina laughed. "You're a strange one, Master Lubos. You were just talking to him a moment ago. Remember, the miller?"

It took a moment for the gears in Lubos' head to mesh together. "Rademaker, the miller, is your father?"

"You don't see the family resemblance? I know I look a lot like my mother. Ah, but you know that already."

Lubos felt himself reddening again. "I thought you were his wife. The one who designed the waterwheels."

"No, that was definitely my mother. Her mother designed the first one, but it was Mother who replaced it with something much more suitable. I've improved on them a little, but there's little I can do there. It's the potential of what we can do with them that I want to work with. But Lord Bachmeier won't hear a word of it."

"Lord Bachmeier said he wanted to marry

you." Lubos wasn't sure why he said it, but he did recognise the wave of jealousy rising up at the thought.

"Do you think me a fool for refusing?"

Her dark eyes seemed to see right through him. It should have made him feel uncomfortable, but Lubos raised his own eyes to meet her gaze. "No. He doesn't deserve a woman like you."

"Meaning he deserves better? Oh, you do have a way with words, Master Lubos. No wonder you're still a bachelor." She walked out.

"No, wait!" Lubos followed her, and seized her shoulder. "Please, Mistress Molina. That is not what I meant. Bachmeier is a fool, with a head as empty as his daughters'. A woman like you would be wasted on the likes of him."

Molina glanced at his hand, but did not shrug out of his grasp. "For once, we agree. Tell me something, as you seem to have untied your tongue. Did you really come here to see the mill? Do you really want the tour my father is so set that I take you on?"

Lubos swallowed. "I came here to see you,

and return the drawing you left up at the pools yesterday. I want to see…anything you're willing to show me. I know I've been a fool, but I wish to show you I am not as much of a fool as Bachmeier. If these waterwheels are truly as useful as you say, then I must tell the king about them."

"Good. Then I'll take you on a tour. My father thought I would have to seduce you and make you marry me before you'd agree to take word of these waterwheels to the capital."

Lubos froze, entranced at the thought of her seducing him. He wanted nothing more.

But she was already striding away, toward the spinning waterwheels, and he had to run to catch up. He didn't intend to lose her this time.

Twelve

A man who blushed! The sensible part of Molina's brain told her to run far and fast from this man, for she had no patience for fools. But the other part of her mind, the louder part, reminded her that everybody did foolish things on occasion. The village boys in particular, when courting a girl they fancied. Not that Lubos could fancy her after such a short time. Then again, she knew he fancied taking her to bed.

She wondered if his being a bigger man would make such a thing better or worse. Not that she intended to try him out just to sate her curiosity. Then who would be the foolish one?

Molina explained how the waterwheels worked, then pointed out the improvements she'd made. They might be small, but they were nevertheless important changes that her mother would surely have made herself, in time.

"And what of the machine you sketched yesterday?" Lubos asked, holding out the damp bark piece that had survived his dunking.

Molina took the drawing and stared at it for a long moment. "An idea that came to me yesterday. A wheel for spinning thread. By making the spinning go faster, a woman could spin more in a day, or have more time for other things. Or if every woman in town had one, and spent the same amount of time spinning, there'd be more linen than they could possibly need. Enough to sell, for there is always a market for linen, whether 'tis coarse or fine. Or if I could harness a waterwheel to power the spinning wheel, or a dozen spinning wheels, much like I've done with the hammers for beating the flax into fibres we can spin..."

Only now did she recognise the glazed over look in Lubos' eyes, and stopped. Maybe he wasn't so different to the village boys or Bachmeier after all. "I can see I'm boring you, Master Lubos."

He shook his head, and the glazed look vanished. "No, you are distracting me. I should be listening to your words, but you're filled with such passion that my thoughts drifted…elsewhere. I must apologise, Mistress Molina. No matter how intently I listen to your words, I will never be able to convey them as clearly as you can. Your ideas are…amazing. They cannot be allowed to rot in this place, like flax in the millponds. They must be conveyed to the king, while they are still fresh and new. When I leave for the capital, you must come with me."

Leave the village and visit the capital? Molina's heart leaped at the thought. No one left the village, and if they did, it was only to visit the next town over. The capital…why, it was as distant as the moon to most of them. To think she might get to meet the king, and have one of the king's own men speaking in support of her…perhaps her spinning wheels could be more than just a dream.

She seized Lubos's shoulders and kissed him. She intended it to be a chaste kiss – she knew her father was watching, after all – but the moment her lips touched his, she forgot everything. His lips were warm and willing, parting to tempt her inside, and she could not refuse. His tongue caressed hers with an ardour that spoke of more, far more, than a simple kiss. And as she kissed him back, letting her tongue dance with his, her body ached to share that ardour, pressing against him so that she could feel the heat of him through his borrowed clothes. What would it feel like to have his hands stroke her the way he'd stroked himself, crying out her name as he touched her…

Molina pushed him away before she tore his clothes off in her passion to satisfy her curiosity.

Molina took a deep breath. "I will come with you," she said, then added, "If my father agrees he can spare me." She nodded up the mountain, to the trees where she suspected her father watched, unseen, waiting for just such a kiss.

She was not surprised, when the question was put to her father, that he sat there as satisfied as a cream-filled cat as he gave his permission. "But you must swear to take good care of her, for Molina is my only daughter, and very precious to me," Father finished.

Lubos looked grave, then placed his hand over his heart. "Sir, I swear to you on my honour that I will hold her life dearer than my own for every moment she is in my care."

Neither made any mention of her returning home, Molina noticed, but chose to hold her tongue. Father imagined her marrying the man, she was sure of it, but Lubos…she wasn't sure why he would want to keep her. Perhaps to supervise the wheel building or some such thing. For a man who could resist Bachmeier's daughters was not one who allowed his passions to rule him.

She pushed away the small voice in her head that protested about how little she knew about this man, or the king and his court. This was her fate, and she would not let such an opportunity pass by without seizing it. No one could know the future, but she knew hers was twisted up with Lubos, at least for now.

And on the journey, she would have time to find out if he truly was a fool, or merely a fool in love. Was it too much to ask that her heart longed for the second?

Thirteen

It took every ounce of Abraham's will not to take Maja in her arms and kiss her like he wanted to. If he failed, he would never see her again. Never touch her…

He dropped to one knee. "My lady, I swear on my life, that I will not return until the curse is broken."

She reached for his face, but he reared back before she could touch his skin. He could not risk her falling victim to his curse.

Tears coursed down her cheeks. "You don't know he has it. You don't. Stay until the babe is born. Then, if he is cursed, as you say, you can go and seek out this witch in the capital. Please, Abraham…"

He shook his head. "You do not understand. The curse will not show until he is close to the end of his life, and then it will be too late. For him. For me. I must find this witch in the capital, for she is in danger, the seer said, and only she can break the curse. I swore an oath to my father on his deathbed. An oath I cannot break."

"What about your oath to love and protect me?"

He met her anguished eyes, and it felt like his heart had been replaced with her own, for anguish squeezed his just the same. But he could not yield. So he swallowed, and said, "This is the only way I can protect you and the child you carry. As long as I am near you, one touch could kill you. I cannot let that happen. Farewell, Maja."

He turned, hardening his heart against the heartbroken sobbing behind him, and strode out to his waiting horse.

"You're a fool," Chase said, emerging from

the shadows outside the gate.

Abraham sighed. "That I am. If I could have spared her this, I would have. Now…I will do all I can to save our son from the curse." He swallowed, wincing as his chest ached again. "Take care of her for me, brother."

"I am her brother, not yours. And a fool, too, for not protecting her from you."

"Then I am honoured to have been able to call you brother, if only for a short time," Abraham said. For in his heart, he knew he would never see Chase or Maja again. Though he would have given everything he owned to be wrong.

With a heavy heart, he spurred his horse into a gallop, leaving behind his home and everything he held dear.

Fourteen

For the first few days, Molina and Lubos rode together on the same palfrey, sometimes with her before him and sometimes behind. They made slow progress, for he stopped often to relieve himself, or so he said. More than once, she'd had to wait for him for some time while he disappeared into the woods, and she grew suspicious, for he drank no more than she did.

On the third morning, he procured a second palfrey from the inn, which he insisted was her new mount, and she was so busy managing the fine-looking but ill-tempered horse she paid little attention to what Lubos did, though it seemed to her he stopped less frequently.

The evenings did not change, though. Especially the ones they spent in the woods, between inns. At least, not until they travelled further north, where the nights were colder. One such night she woke up, shivering, despite her heavy cloak and the merrily burning fire.

"Is it always so cold, Master Lubos?" she asked through chattering teeth.

"Yes," he said gravely. "I must find you a fur cloak before winter, for you will need it in the capital. In the meantime, you may share mine." He flipped open his fur-lined cloak in invitation.

Molina hesitated for only a moment before she accepted. Rolled up in her own cloak, she was soon enveloped in his, too. Close enough to kiss him, yet separated by enough layers of linen and wool to ensure propriety.

Each night in the open, it became an oft-repeated routine. He would vanish into the woods for a little while, then return and offer to share his cloak with her. More than one morning, she'd woken in his arms, with her head resting on his shoulder or his chest. Neither of them spoke of it, but it seemed like a small enough thing, so Molina didn't mind if he didn't.

One night, when Lubos took his usual walk into the woods, Molina thought she heard him call her name. Then again, with considerable urgency. She hurried after him, determined to help him if he needed her.

But she found he did not need her help at all, for it was as though they were back in her father's house, with him holding his manhood in both hands as he said her name, over and over.

This was what he did every night, and every morning, too, Molina realised. So she wasn't the only one having carnal thoughts when they lay together at night.

"Do all men exercise their manhoods as often as you do?" Molina burst out, unable to restrain her curiosity any more. "Or is it because yours is bigger that it requires more exercise than most?"

Lubos turned and stared at her, his face reddening. Had he truly thought she didn't know what he was doing?

"I mean, every night and again every morning seems a little excessive. Most of the men in the village only do it once a night, which is once more than their wives would like, or so they say. Yet here you are, at it again."

"I can't stop thinking about you. Even in my dreams. This…helps." He turned away and resumed stroking himself.

The idea came again, the one that she couldn't stop thinking about, and this time Molina didn't dismiss it. Instead, she said, "What would you be willing to give me if I…if I helped you?"

She almost laughed at her own awkward words. How her father believed she could seduce anyone, she didn't know. But she could not forget that kiss, or the thoughts that had come after.

"Helped me how?"

She gritted her teeth. She'd have to say it now. "If I were to lift my skirts, perch on your lap, and let you put that snake of yours inside me?"

He let out a shaky breath. "I…I'd give everything I have. My heart, my love, my protection for as long as I live. I'd marry you, make you my bride, and love you all the days of my life. But I'd want you more than just once, Molina. I'd want you always."

Always, as he loved her all the days of his life. Some sort of madness descended on her, or perhaps it was sanity. She wasn't sure. But Molina marched up to Lubos and straddled him, lifting her skirts so she could feel his skin against hers. She looked deep into his eyes. "Swear it," she said.

He groaned. "Oh, Molina, I'd make you my wife before I dared do this. Yes, I swear by my life and yours and all I hold dear. I will marry you, if you are willing."

"Good," she said, then pushed against him, feeling the heat of him as he entered her. He cupped her bottom and drove deep, and she gasped. This was nothing like the one quick fumble she'd had with Rikard. Not painful at all. This was…wonderful. "I'll marry you, on one condition," she said breathlessly.

"Name it," he panted.

"You must make love to me every night. Just like this."

He laughed. "It shall be as my lady wishes. Every night."

Her pleasure built until she could no longer control it. She cried out, clenching down hard on him. The other girls in the village had never told her about this. Maybe this was the courtly love the wandering minstrels sang about, known only to men at court.

"I love you, Lubos," she said.

"And I love you, sweet Molina. I've never seen you more beautiful than you are tonight. I would give anything to hear you scream my name like that again."

The way he moved within her, his soft kisses on her breasts and her face, his arms holding her tight…it was only a matter of time before she granted his wish, screaming his name into the night as she felt his own, blissful release deep inside her. And for the first time in her life, she was content.

Fifteen

Three times he made love to her that first night, and again in the morning. If he'd thought her passion for machines was bewitching, it was nothing compared to the unrestrained joy on her face as he brought her to the peak of her pleasure. Even in his dreams, he hadn't imagined coupling with her could be this good. And now, he couldn't imagine ever loving another woman the way he loved her.

Watching her climb astride her mare shot a pang of jealousy through his heart. He wished he hadn't bought her the horse, so that she might ride before him again, pressed against his groin as she drove him to distraction. For tonight they would spend the night in a fine inn, where they would share the inn's biggest bed, and he could show her how much better he performed in a bed instead of the cold, hard ground. He'd make sure the room had a good fire, so that he could lay her naked upon the bed, and take his time learning every inch of the lovely body he'd touched in the dark last night.

They made good time, perhaps because he'd set a faster pace in his eagerness to arrive at their destination. It was barely mid-afternoon. Perhaps he could persuade her to retire early…

He glanced back at Molina, just in time to see her almost fall out of her saddle, she was so tired. Lubos raced to her side, ready to catch her as she half-slid, half fell off the horse into his arms.

"Innkeep, your best room!" Lubos shouted.

The innkeeper himself came running out, wide-eyed. He recognised Lubos on sight. "Of course. And for…the woman?"

She was more than just some woman. Molina would one day be his queen. "Your best is for Lady Molina, my bride. We have ridden hard for some weeks now, and I fear it is more than she is accustomed to. A warm fire, water to wash with, a good meal, and plenty of rest is what she needs."

The innkeeper bowed low. "Of course. One of my manservants will take her for you, and the grooms will see to your horses. Your father has sent – "

"No one touches her but me," Lubos growled, surprising himself, but not as much as the innkeeper, whose eyes were now wide as saucers.

"As you wish, Your Highness. But your father sent an urgent missive for you, and I dare not disobey the king, whose messenger said I must give it into your hands the moment I saw you."

"When my bride is safe and warm, I will come down, and see to this missive," Lubos said, already ascending the stairs with Molina in his arms.

He laid her on the bed, then knelt to

remove her boots. She had the tiniest feet — how had he not noticed before? He pulled off her stockings, remembering the feel of that fine linen against his back as she wrapped her legs around him.

"Lubos?" Her voice was sleepy and slurred.

He'd kept her up half the night, not letting her sleep at all. And here he was, wanting to interrupt her sleep again with more lovemaking. Lubos cursed himself. He'd have her for the rest of their lives — he could certainly wait an hour or two until she was rested.

"Rest, my lady. We're at an inn. I will make sure no one disturbs you," he said.

She sat up, blinking. "An inn? Is there water I can wash with?"

As if on cue, a maid knocked on the open door and entered, staggering under the weight of two full jugs of water. She was followed by two more girls, each as heavily laden, and a third carrying a wooden tub.

The thought of Molina bathing naked stopped him in his tracks. He should dismiss the maids and offer to help her himself. Then afterwards, perhaps…

"Sir, I was charged to remind you about the letter from the king," one of the maids said, dragging him out of much pleasanter thoughts.

Reluctantly, Lubos nodded. "Duty must come first." He followed the girls down the stairs, leaving Molina alone in her chamber.

His father's missive had been long and suspicious, demanding answers about the various barons Lubos had visited, between lengthy rants about the infractions of each baron, or sometimes even the present baron's ancestors, for Father was a firm believer in bloodlines breeding true to the source. No matter how many times Lubos told him his son was not merely a younger copy of himself.

Sighing, Lubos had called for parchment and ink, and sat down to write the lengthy reply his father required, for it would be some weeks before they arrived in the capital, and Father needed to know his barons were doing their best to recover from the spring floods, as opposed to cheating him of his tithes this year.

Darkness had fallen by the time he was done, and he trudged up the stairs behind a maid bearing their dinner on a tray. She placed it on the table, dropped a curtsey, and left, closing the door behind her.

Molina was asleep, cocooned in the bed like she'd lain in her cloak beside the fire those first few nights, before he'd made his thoughtless offer to share his cloak with her. She'd chosen to unwittingly torture him by accepting.

All those nights, laying beside her and not laying a finger on her, until last night…and now he would share her bed. Dinner could wait, for Lubos could wait no longer. He shucked off his clothes and crawled into bed beside her.

She'd bathed and dressed in a thin shift, so she now smelled faintly of soap and whatever herbs and flowers she kept her linens in. And she was warm, from the combination of the merry blaze and the thick eiderdown that covered her. Almost as warm as she'd been last night…

Lubos reached down, edging up the hem of her shift so that he could stroke her thigh. Her skin was as soft as the silks he'd dress her in, once he got her to the capital. He slid a finger inside her, gasping as he found her as hot and wet as when he'd surrendered to her last night.

She moaned in her sleep. "Mm, Lubos."

He wanted to hear her scream his name again.

He slid a second finger into her, stroking in and out, before pressing his thumb against that tiny little nub that was the centre of her pleasure.

She bucked, moaning louder this time, which only made him stroke harder. Her muscles clenched around his fingers, holding him inside her, as Lubos circled her with his thumb. Her eyes flew open as her back arched up. "Oh my God, Lubos!" she cried out.

He withdrew his drenched fingers, then impulsively stuck them in his mouth, to see if she tasted as sweet as she looked. Ha, she was both sweet and salty, and he wanted more. He spread her legs wide, kissing his way up her thigh before plunging his tongue deep inside her.

God, she tasted good. He slid his fingers inside her again, sucking hard at that little nub of hers until she gasped with delight. Slowly, he took up the same rhythm as before, slower, more sensuously this time, as he relished the taste of her. Then she thrust her hips toward him, much like he'd thrust deep into her last night.

"Lubos, please!" she begged, tangling her fingers in his hair, throwing her legs over his shoulders to give him better access to all of her. "Oh please!"

She came with a scream, her back arching so far off the bed only her head touched it any more.

Before she could come down of her own accord, he seized her around the waist, easing her onto his rock-hard cock. Her heels dug into his back as he drove deep, deeper inside her than he'd ever been before. He filled her completely, his balls resting against her as if clamouring for entry, too. She felt so good, he hoped he wasn't hurting her. He risked a glance at her face.

Her eyes met his. "More," she demanded, clenching down on his cock.

He pressed his thumb against her little nub, hearing her gasp as he slid almost out of her and then right back in, where he belonged. "Be careful what you wish for, my lady," he whispered, keeping his thrusts slow and steady and powerfully deep, until his circling thumb unravelled her once more. He silenced her scream with a kiss, and threw caution to the winds. Slow and steady be damned. He pounded into her, egged on by her breathless commands for more until she clenched around him one more time, crying out his name over and over, and he was undone.

When Lubos managed to open his eyes again, Molina, the most magnificent woman he'd ever met, eased her legs down from his shoulders, to wrap them even more firmly around his waist, holding him deep inside her.

"I am not ready to do that again, my lady. We men do not have the stamina of a lady like you," Lubos apologised.

Molina gave a slight smile. "Perhaps not, but when you are ready, I will be the first to know." And she clenched deliciously around him, making Lubos wish he was ready now.

Some hours later, he awoke to find her sitting astride him, rocking her hips gently as she rubbed against his once more hard cock. Like a dream made real. One who would one day be his wife.

"I want more," she whispered.

Lubos seized her hips, chuckling as she gasped in surprise, and thrust home.

Sixteen

Every night and every blissful morning, Molina had to pry her body from Lubos'. If she didn't, then she would neither sleep nor leave their shared bed, though it was becoming increasingly hard to remember why she wanted to.

But today, Lubos had assured her, they would reach the capital, and she did want to do that. She pawed through her clothes, wanting something clean, but she'd worn all of them on this long trip. The only item that had stayed in her bag was her red petticoat, for her moonblood had not come this month. That meant she carried Lubos' child already. Good. Once they were married, they would be a family all the sooner. So much for the village boys' taunts that she was so thin, she must be barren. Or a witch, as though her skills with the waterwheels were some kind of magic and not simply something that came naturally to her mind.

Lubos wanted waterwheels and whatever she wanted to show him. And her. Oh, how he wanted her. Even this morning his loving smile melted something inside her.

"Come back to bed," he said.

She shook her head. "We enter the capital today. I want to wear my best, but everything is so travel worn, I fear I shall look like your poor country cousin."

He rose and kissed her. "You will look beautiful, as always, no matter what you wear. And you shall have all new clothes in the latest court fashions, if that is your wish. Nothing is too good for my lovely wife."

"When will we be married? Will there be enough time to have a new gown made, or to launder these?" Molina asked.

"You shall name the day. I must report to the king first, but after that, my time is yours."

"As I am yours." She melted into his arms, wishing her worries would melt just as easily. Every inn they stopped at, he proudly introduced her as his new bride, and Molina wanted to believe him with all her might. But her mind would not stop spinning with all the things that could possibly go wrong.

Seventeen

"I should change my gown before I see the king," Molina said, hanging back even as Lubos seized her hand to lead her into the throne room.

Lubos shook his head. "It's best not to delay when reporting to the king. He is very insistent about being the first to know any news. And he will not notice your gown, I promise you. Why, I can't tell if it's the same gown you wore yesterday, or if it is a new one. The only thing he would notice about your gown is if you weren't wearing one, because no man is immune to your beauty."

Molina blushed. "You should not say such things. I'm sure if I had any beauty to boast of, someone in my village would have noticed and told me of it. And he will notice this gown, I am sure of it, for I left half of the skirt in a bramble hedge beside the road when that hateful horse decided to scratch her flank against it. Why, it is nothing but ribbons all down one side!"

When she held it out, Lubos realised the gown was quite ruined, but the layer of cloth beneath seemed unharmed, as were her stockings. Her modesty would be preserved.

"I didn't notice until you told me. I'm sure he won't, either. Here, I shall walk on that side of you as we enter the throne room, and it will be quite invisible." Before she could object again, Lubos linked his arm through hers and marched into the throne room.

Courtiers passed to let them through, bowing as they recognised him. Lubos wanted to point out to Molina that nobody noticed a little dust from the road, that they saw him for who he was, and it would be the same for her, but he kept his observations for later. The sooner this audience was over, the better.

He stopped at the foot of the dais and bowed low. "Father, you will not believe what I found in Lord Bachmeier's barony."

"The skinniest, ugliest whore in the kingdom?"

Lubos heard Molina's gasp as her hand slipped from his grasp.

Father didn't seem to have noticed. "Bachmeier said he had the most beautiful daughters in the country. Plump, fair and fertile – just what any man would want in a wife. If that beanpole is one of his, then what else has he lied about?"

Lubos rose. "Father, this is Lady Molina, and she is most certainly not one of Bachmeier's daughters, though the man wanted to marry her himself. She works miracles. The things she can do with waterwheels and a wheel for spinning thread…why, if we equipped every mill in the country with one of her wheels, the treasury would be full of gold within the year. Never have I seen anything like it. Machines that can do the work of three men, using the water from the river! If you let me show you…"

The king waved his hand languidly. "I have no desire to see what some slovenly stable girl can do. I'm sure she has spread her legs and her lies far enough, for you to have been ensnared by her. Has she fucked away your wits, too, so that I will need to name your brother Xylander the crown prince instead of you?"

Lubos didn't dare look at Molina. All he knew was he had to get her out of there.

"Your Majesty will choose his successor wisely, I am certain," Lubos said evenly. "Just as you have chosen your loyal barons and lords wisely, for they have striven mightily to provide you with a tithe even in these times of hardship and floods, which took most of their harvests. As you will have already seen in the reports I sent back while I was travelling. And as you were kind enough to bring up the subject of marriage, I would very much like to discuss my marriage with you, though perhaps in the privacy of your apartments…" He glanced pointedly at the packed court behind him.

"There is nothing to discuss. As long as she is female and fertile and of a rank befitting your station, and she comes with a sizeable dowry in gold, you may bed whatever bitch you please. When the sow is pregnant, then you may go back to tumbling stable girls." Father made a shooing motion with his hands. "Get this slut out of my sight."

Lubos muttered something he hoped sounded obedient and suitably contrite, before hustling Molina out. He almost had to carry her, for her feet didn't seem to want to work until the throne room door had closed behind them.

"I must apologise for my father. His mind is not as sharp as it was," Lubos began, but Molina didn't seem to hear him.

He'd been such a fool. Gently, he took her hand and guided her to his chambers, where he could apologise to her properly without half the court hearing.

Eighteen

Molina's mind whirled worse than ever. Lubos was the crown prince. His father, the king, wanted nothing to do with waterwheels and wouldn't let them marry, for he thought she was unworthy of his princely son. Far from home, carrying Lubos' child…what was she to do?

She followed Lubos through the castle, as lost in her own thoughts as in the maze of stone halls.

Lubos opened another door and gestured for her to go through. When Molina did, she found herself in a tower room, instead of another passage. A bedchamber, if she didn't miss her guess, full of the sort of rich furnishings she would expect to belong to royalty.

Not at all suitable for the…what had the king called her? Oh yes: the slovenly stable girl who had spread her legs and her lies for the prince. Lovely. Bachmeier's snide comments about her sanity seemed almost like compliments in comparison.

"I'll have some water sent up, and a maid with fresh clothes, who will see that yours are laundered. I'll have some dinner sent up, too, for my father's great hall is not the place for you yet, I think. Not until we are wed," Lubos said.

Molina laid a hand on his arm. "When we are wed? Why, did you not hear the king? He said he would never allow us to wed. Lubos, Your Highness, I cannot allow you to commit treason. You cannot lose your head for me." And she would lose hers, too, she thought but didn't say.

Lubos grimaced. "My father is old and

prone to rash decisions, like today, but, in time, I have found he will eventually see reason. So he will over our marriage. He sent me out to find gold from his vassals, and a bride. He made no mention of wealth or dowries then, and once his ire has cooled, I will explain to him the value of your waterwheels. Then, he will demand we marry, and we will. Until then, remain here in my quarters as much as possible, except when you are working with the castle carpenter. Or is it the wainwright you need? Whoever and whatever you need, you shall have it, so that when my father wishes to speak to you again, you will have not just a picture but a real, moving device to show him."

Against her better judgement, hope kindled in Molina's breast. "These are your quarters?"

"Yes, and they will be yours, too. As my bride to be, you will be showed all the respect befitting a princess. New gowns, new shoes, a new spinning wheel…all that you ask for will be yours. Even me, for I made a vow I intend to keep." He pulled her into his arms and kissed the top of her head. "Please, be patient just a little while, my love, and everything will be as it should be. I promise." He pulled away and bowed to her. "A maid, water, dinner...I shall have it all sent up to you on my way to see the carpenter. Then I will return to share the meal with you, before we retire to bed for the night. If that meets with your approval, my lady."

Now who was struck dumb? The irony wasn't lost on her. "I...yes," she said finally. "Your Highness," she added.

He waved the words away. "There are no titles between us. You are my lady, and my equal. In my mind, you are already my bride. Anything else is just mere words and ceremony. I am yours. Never doubt that." Then he whirled on his heel and was gone.

Molina sat on the enormous bed – big enough for Lubos and all four of Bachmeier's daughters, if he'd chosen all of the girls, instead of just her – and tried to calm her thoughts. With all her heart, she wanted to believe Lubos. She placed a hand on her belly. For the future of the child inside her, she had to hope what he said was true.

In the meantime, she would work with this carpenter, and do everything Lubos said. For this court was a strange place to her, as alien as the surface of the moon, and one wrong step would see her lose not just her own life, but her child's life, too. Molina swore it would not come to that.

Nineteen

Lubos found Zimmerman in his workshop outside the castle gates. He watched the carpenter hammering what looked like a chair before Zimmerman noticed him.

Down went the hammer and Zimmerman bowed. "Your Highness. An honour."

It hadn't always been an honour. Zimmerman had often chased Lubos and the castellan's boys out of his workshop when they came searching for wood to make into toy boats to sail on the moat. Lubos grinned. "Do you have any spare bits for boats, Master

Zimmerman?"

Zimmerman's mouth dropped open. "I'd forgotten about you boys and those boats. It seems like so long ago…but Your Highness has only to ask, and I will make whatever you wish. Though if it's boats you're after, might I suggest Bootsma, the royal boatbuilder instead? As I'm sure you and your friends found out all too quickly, my fresh planks are more likely to sink than float."

"It's not for me, my friend. I need your skills for my fiancée, the amazing woman I'll soon marry. She has the most…inventive mind, contraptions that could do the work of a man or a woman, or even a whole village. Using wheels and water and all manner of things. Truly remarkable. What Lady Molina designs, I want you to build for her. I need you to bring her drawings to life, so that my father can truly appreciate them."

Zimmerman sucked in a breath. "So the rumours are true! People have been spreading stories, that you'd found a bride somewhere in the provinces, and you were bringing her home. Some even said she had the next heir on the way."

Molina, carrying his child? He couldn't imagine a happier thought. Well, they'd certainly made love enough times on the journey for such a thing to happen, though it was probably too early to know.

"She is like no other woman I've ever met. A treasure who will one day be queen. In the meantime, I'm sure she will keep you and every other carpenter in the kingdom busy improving the place. Now would be a good time to take on an apprentice or two."

Zimmerman bowed. "It will be an honour to work for the future queen. Something to tell my grandkids, if my daughters ever get around to having any."

"That it will be," Lubos promised him, before heading back into the castle.

He found his father in his private chambers, dressing for dinner, as usual at this time of day. "What do you want?" Father demanded. "Come to tell me you've gone and married the stable girl against my wishes, so I'll have to cut off her head? Don't test me, boy – I'll do it, no matter how pretty she is. Our treasury needs gold, not girls."

"I'll bring you the gold you ask for, Father, you'll see. Many of the provinces were hard hit by the spring floods, and they have little to spare. But what I discovered out there…ah, you should have seen it, Father. They were using the floodwaters to power the millwheels, and to make linen, and all manner of things. Almost miraculous. I'll ask Zimmerman to put together some models so that you can see these things in action. I'm sure you'll see how useful they will be. For while a machine mills the grain, the men can plant another crop. Triple the size of the usual flax crop, ready to spin into linen thread in half the time it normally takes." Lubos almost added that it was all thanks to Molina, but held his tongue. When his father saw the models and truly appreciated their value, then he would tell the king that she alone was responsible for them.

Father squinted at him. "I thought you said the girl made them?"

"She designs them. A skilled carpenter has to make them," Lubos said. Actually, he wouldn't put it past Molina to have done the work herself back at home. But she had no need for such things here. Providing for her was his job now.

"I will see the models when you have them. Until then – where are my tithe collectors with my gold? Aren't you supposed to be with them?"

Lubos sighed. His father forgot far too much these days. "Molina and I rode ahead to bring you the news. I will return to the cart train on the morrow to see if I can hurry them along." Not likely, but it was what his father wanted to hear.

"Good. Can't leave you a penniless kingdom when my reign is over, can I? What kind of king would that make me?"

Lubos made suitably sympathetic noises, but inside, his resolve was as hard as iron. With or without his father's help, he and Molina would work to make their kingdom great again. As husband and wife.

Twenty

Abraham reined in his horse just before the bridge. With all the traffic headed into the city, including an endless train of carts that looked to be carrying either the king's tithe or enough food to feed an army, he hadn't been moving faster than a walk anyway, but now he had to stop, for the very tower the witch had spoken about loomed above him.

The windows were unshuttered in the warm summer air, and Abraham fancied he could see a shape looking out through one. A feminine silhouette, there for a moment, before it was gone.

A maiden locked in the tower, perhaps? One who would be so grateful to him for rescuing her that she would break the curse as a matter of course?

It would not be easy getting in, for the tower was part of the castle, but that was where his magic shoes would come in. He would sneak in, carry the girl out, persuade her to break the curse, and be home with Maja before the baby was born.

He would hold his son in his arms, free of the curse that had plagued their bloodline for far too long, or he would not be able to look his son in the eye, for he would be a failure of a father.

Abraham urged his horse across the bridge, his eyes fixed on the tower. Therein lay his salvation, and he would not let it slip from his grasp.

Twenty-One

Molina rose and peered out the window. Ever since the morning Lubos left, she'd been watching for him. While she worked with Zimmerman, she'd managed to put him out of her mind for an hour or two at a time, but now she had the thread spinning wheel and spindle arrangement before her, she was terrified to try it. What if it worked? What if it didn't? This was sleeker, more polished than the simple device she'd imagined, but then she hadn't expected to have the services of a royal carpenter who made ornate carved chairs for his living.

She squinted at a horseman on the bridge, but he didn't look like Lubos. She'd ridden beside Lubos enough to recognise him on sight. Yet the carts coming through the gate were more numerous than usual, so they had to be the tithe. Where was Lubos, then?

Perhaps he was even now on his way up to the tower to surprise her.

She turned away from the window, smiling. She could surprise him, too. The baby was a visible bump between her hips now, and she had this table thing. Which she had to test before he got here, for if it worked…

She found some combed flax, as fluffy as fresh-combed wool, and twisted a length of it into thread between her fingers, threading it on the spindle. When she'd secured it, she set the fluffy flax on the distaff, and gave the wheel a push with her elbow. The spindle spun and she soon had her hands full, keeping the wheel turning while she twisted the thread. If the wheel could be spun by water or even her foot, it would be much better, but she was slowly getting accustomed to this. The spindle was full almost before she realised it, and she fitted a second. This time, she spun the wheel a little faster, for she had the timing of it, and the second spindle was full in no time. Why, she'd barely been working for a few minutes, and she'd done a whole morning's work.

This would change everything.

She wanted to shout and dance and sing, but she didn't dare do any of these things in the king's castle until Lubos returned, for he should be the first one to know. So she fitted her third and final spindle, and began to spin again.

As if in answer to her wish, the door behind her swung open and the footsteps that entered were too heavy to belong to anyone but a man. Lubos was home.

"Come and see," she said. "It's even better than I imagined it could be." She didn't dare stop, for the thread would be uneven.

A hand descended on her spindle, stopping it. "Lady, you need to stop playing with that toy. For what I have to say to you is a matter of life or death if you do not." He let go of her spindle, but it no longer moved, for he'd done something to the thread that turned it yellow.

Molina stared up in horror…at a man who certainly wasn't Lubos.

Twenty-Two

The terrified girl seemed to banish her fear in a moment as she rose. "Who are you?" she demanded.

She was a princess, the seer had said, which explained her regal bearing, as well as her fine gown. Maja had nothing half so fine. Abraham promised himself that when the curse was broken, he would find a fabric merchant to sell him some rich cloth to take home as a gift for Maja.

But first he had to persuade the girl to help him, and not betray him to the king. For the king would not look kindly upon an intruder in his castle, however loyal the House of Rumpelstiltskin might be.

"Who I am matters not," Abraham said finally. "All that matters is you help me."

She edged away from him, toward the door. "You should not be here. If you wish for someone's help, you should petition the king." Her hand closed on the door handle.

"No!" Abraham shouted, lunging for her.

She scrambled away, crossing the room so that the wheeled table she had been playing with stood between them. "If my husband returns and finds you here, he will cut you down. Leave while you still have legs to run with. For if you harm me, there is nowhere you can run to where he will not find you."

Harm her? He had to save her!

Abraham stared at her for a long moment before he could find the words he needed. "I have not come here to hurt you, Princess," he said slowly. "I need your help, and I will pay handsomely for it. So handsomely, you will never need to spin your own thread again." He reached for the spindles of spun thread he recognised, for Maja had used similar ones, and closed his fingers around them. In a moment, the common white thread turned to pure gold. He held out the transformed spindles. "You see?"

"What have you done?" she demanded.

"I will make you richer than you have ever dreamed, if only you help me," Abraham said. He thought he heard footsteps on the stairs. He would have to be quick. "Come with me. I will tell you everything you need to know, and once you have helped me, I will fill your chamber with enough gold to last you a lifetime."

"I don't want gold or riches. I want my husband, and no one else. Get out!" she said fiercely.

The footsteps were getting closer. "Please, Princess!" Abraham pulled on his gloves and offered her his hand. "All the wealth you could ever want, and all I ask is a night of your time."

"No!"

The door handle moved. Abraham was out of time.

"I shall return on the morrow, and ask you

again," he promised, before stamping his foot three times to conjure a hole large enough for him to escape through before the door opened.

Twenty-Three

Lubos wanted to skip all the way up to her chamber, as she'd named the empty room above his own that Molina had claimed for her workroom. He settled for racing up the steps, something he hadn't done since he was a boy.

He threw open the door, and there she was. For a moment, she seemed transfixed with shock, before her thunderous expression cleared and her beaming smile blinded him.

"Lubos!" She dashed across the room and threw her arms around him, kissing him with such fervour he wished he'd thought to commission a bed for this chamber.

He did not want to break the embrace, but he knew he would have to. His father expected him in the throne room, and he would have to explain his delay.

Gently, he pushed her away from him so that she stood at arm's length. "I must report to the king, and I cannot take you with me. Not yet." One day, he promised himself.

"No, not yet." She wrapped her arms around herself and shivered, though the room was not cold. The king had that effect on many people, it seemed.

Lubos cast around the room, and his gaze lit upon the wheeled table he'd seen in her drawings. "Did Zimmerman manage to make one for you? Does it work?"

She smiled. "It took several tries, but yes, he finished this for me today. I sat down to spin, and it seemed but a moment, yet I did a whole day's work in that time. I've never spun so much in my life. Spinning with a wheel is easily twice or thrice as fast as spinning by hand. Look how many spindles I filled." She waved a hand at the table, and the pile of what Lubos had to assume were spindles.

Lubos gathered them up, then kissed her quickly. "I'll take these to my father, and tell him you have a machine that can make miracles. I'm sure it will please him. I told you we will help him see reason."

Before he could surrender to his desire for her again, he forced his feet to carry him out of her chamber. "Once I have reported to the king, I am yours, my lady. I have a great number of kisses I mean to share with you, in our bedchamber below," he called over his shoulder as he headed down the stairs.

"I will be waiting," he heard her say.

Grinning, Lubos marched to the throne room, only to find his father had dismissed the court for the day. Sighing, he headed back up a different set of stairs to his father's solar.

He heard his father's muttering before he entered the room, and strained his ears to hear the words. Something about demanding his son for marriage, when he'd offered his daughter. His father didn't sound likely to accept the proposal, whoever it was for, and Lubos breathed a sigh of relief.

"Good evening, Father," he said loudly, as he entered the solar. No courtly bows were required here, for there was no audience to impress.

"Is it?" Father eyed the window suspiciously. "Have you caught my thieving barons yet, boy?"

Lubos shook his head. "No, not yet. They all seem to be a loyal lot. But I do bring good news. Lady Molina has perfected the miraculous spinning wheel she promised, and look what she has made!" He set the three spindles on the table before his father.

They didn't look particularly impressive. For a moment, Lubos wished he'd brought Molina and her spinning wheel along, too, but then he remembered his father's tastes ran to women like Bachmeier's daughters, not his lithe lady.

Father picked one up and examined it, then took it to the window, where the sunlight might better illuminate Molina's work.

"Who did this?" Father demanded.

"Lady Molina, the lady I wish to marry," Lubos began.

"How?" Father interrupted.

"With a miraculous spinning wheel of her own design. She takes some combed flax, spins the wheel, twists the flax through her fingers, and turns it into that. Faster than you can believe," Lubos said proudly.

"She shall show me on the morrow. If it is truly as you say, you must marry the girl. Marry her, before someone else does."

Lubos hardly dared believe his luck. "Marry her on the morrow? Father, thank you!"

Father glared at him. "I did not say that. Tomorrow she will prove her claims, while you finish the quest I have twice sent you on, but you have failed at. When you have found the barons cheating me of my share, and restored their tithe to me, then you may marry her. Meantime, I shall keep her close. She cannot be allowed to escape. Make sure you lock her in her chambers tonight."

There would be no need to lock her in anywhere, Lubos thought but didn't say. He could happily keep Molina confined to the bed until the morrow, and she would be his willing prisoner. Especially when he told her he had his father's permission to marry on his return.

He bade his father a good evening for the second time, and sped to the chamber where Molina waited for him.

Twenty-Four

The moment the bedchamber door closed behind him, Molina opened her mouth to share all her worries with Lubos, not least of all the strange man who'd stopped her spinning wheel, but Lubos pressed a finger to her lips.

"I must leave in the morning, to finish my quest for the king. The sooner I go, the sooner I may return and we can be married. I know you have much to tell me — I could tell you much about my travels, too — but neither is important right now. We have one night together, and I wish to spend it sharing as much love as possible, so that the memory will warm us both when we are far apart." He looked longingly into her eyes. "I will make love to you any way you wish, from now until dawn, and I swear the next night we spend together shall be our wedding night. My father has agreed, and so it shall be."

The very thought of him inside her once more kindled a fire within her brighter than she'd imagined possible. Why, it seemed her insides burned to feel him again. Lubos was right. She didn't want to waste these precious hours with words.

She hitched up her skirt, layers of silk and linen, until she was bare to the waist, but for her stockings. She hooked one leg around his hip, sliding her hand up under his tunic for his hard length. Her fingers tangled with his, intent on one purpose — uniting them. He thrust inside her, cupping her bottom as he lifted her, pushing deeper to her moaning satisfaction.

"Oh God, Molina," he said as he backed her up against the wall. "So long I've been dreaming of you like this."

She fastened her legs around his hips, holding his gaze as he filled her. "And I you. Make the first time hard and fast. If we have all night, we can take our time."

He chuckled. "Hard and fast you shall have, but I think you have forgotten something. My lady must come first." He pinned her to the wall, as full of him as she was with child. Without taking his eyes off hers, his thumb found precisely the right spot at the apex of her thighs, rubbing hard and fast until her vision dissolved into stars. Only then did he move again, maintaining the same rhythm until they cried out for joy together.

She was too busy gasping for breath to protest when he withdrew from her. But then he carried her to bed, and began to unlace her gown. He peeled away layers of fabric until he'd bared her breasts, which he covered with kisses. With her nipples already far too sensitive, thanks to her pregnancy, the moment he decided to suck on one was almost enough to send her over the edge, and she cried out.

"Did I hurt you?" he asked immediately,

pulling away.

"No, of course not. Please, don't stop," she said.

He grinned and lowered his lips to her breast again. His hands dipped lower, bunching her skirts up until he'd bared her legs. Legs she parted willingly at a touch, for she knew the magic that dwelled in his fingers. Magic that soon made her cry out his name, over and over, until she was too hoarse to speak.

Only then did he finish undressing her, dragging her skirts down and throwing them to the floor, heedless of what happened to them. When she wore nothing but her silken stockings, he paused.

"Would you like me to take them off?" she asked, feeling incredibly self-conscious as his eyes devoured her otherwise naked body.

"No. They stay," he said, sitting on the bed beside her. "Now, come sit in my lap and help me take my clothes off."

He didn't wait for a response, lifting her easily so that she sat astride him, just like on their very first time together. And he was rock hard between her thighs, ready for her. She reached down, ready to guide him inside her, but Lubos caught her hands and lifted them to the buttons at the front of his tunic. "I'll take care of that. You see to my clothes."

Her hands shaking with anticipation, she worked at the fastenings on his tunic. Never had it taken her so long to free three buttons from their loops, and she almost cried when the third one finally came free. As if that was his cue, Lubos thrust into her partway, holding tight to her hips when she tried to squirm down the length of him to drive him deeper inside her. "My clothes," he reminded her.

Reluctantly, she pulled his tunic up over his head.

He slid in an inch deeper.

She took a deep breath, tugging his under tunic off, too.

He filled her completely and she let out a sigh of pleasure.

"Don't forget my hose," he said, grinning.

Molina glanced over her shoulder. Sure enough, he wore thick woollen hose, the cloth scratchy beneath her bottom. Yes, they had to go. She managed to get them down past his knees by rising up onto her own knees, but in order to pull them off entirely she'd need to lean right back. One glance at his grin told her he had no intention of helping.

Wrapping her legs securely around his waist, she bent backward, arching her back up as she stretched her arms behind her to push his hose down his calves and off his feet.

"My God, you're beautiful, Molina." His finger stroked the nipple of one upthrust breast. A delicious sensation that made her cry out again. "Here, I'll help you up." One strong hand splayed across her back, while his other fastened around her hip, crushing her against him. But instead of lifting her up, he fell back on the mattress, pulling her with him until she sat astride him while he lay supine on the bed. "If I had a choice, I would spend every moment of the rest of my life like this with you. Hard and deep inside you, while you ride me to the peak of your own pleasure, with your breasts bouncing just like that." With his hands on her hips, he lifted and lowered her, thrusting up to meet her until she caught his rhythm, leaving his hands free to caress her breasts until she screamed.

But they didn't stop.

Not until dawn stole him from her, and she collapsed, empty and aching, in his lonely bed. For nothing was quite as heartbreaking as holding her husband to be and losing him, all in one night.

Twenty-Five

"Get her up and dressed. Now!"

The male voice giving orders wasn't one Molina recognised. But when unfamiliar hands seized her arms and dragged her from her bed, it no longer mattered.

"Unhand me!" she demanded. "Do you know what Prince Lubos will say if he discovers you have laid hands on his bethrothed?"

"Nothing good, I'm sure, but it doesn't matter, miss, for my orders come from the king."

Someone threw open the window shutters and Molina blinked in the bright light. The man who'd spoken, giving orders that came from the king, was the king's guard captain, who'd stood at the king's side in court. A man of honour, or so she'd thought.

He caught sight of her, too, and turned his back. "Avert your eyes, men, and let the lady dress!"

His men obeyed, and Molina hurried to don the clothes Lubos had stripped from her last night. Dropped from the very heights of passion to this rude awakening.

When she was decently covered, she asked, "Where are you taking me?" She did her best to hide her dread at what the captain might answer.

"To another room in the castle, where the king wants you to demonstrate your spinning skills. When your work is done, I have orders to return you to the prince's chambers."

That didn't sound so bad. Spinning for a day was no harder than what she did at home. Molina managed to summon her best smile as she pulled on her boots. "Then shall we go,

Captain?"

He nodded, looking relieved, and gestured for his men to follow behind them. He led her to an older part of the castle, with narrower passageways and uneven stairs leading ever upward, until he opened the door to another tower room, nowhere near as handsomely furnished as the prince's. No tapestries adorned these walls, and his bed would not have fitted here. The windows were little more than arrow slits, where they were visible at all, for the walls were stacked high with baskets of flax, waiting to be spun.

In the middle of all this sat her spinning wheel, fitted with a new spindle. A box containing dozens more sat on a stool that was evidently where she was expected to sit while she laboured.

It would be a challenge, but she suspected that with the aid of her wheel, she could have it all spun before the day was done. If not…well, it wasn't as though Lubos waited for her. The bed would be cold without him, so what was an evening's work if she had little else to do?

She thanked the captain and set to work, barely noticing when the door closed, so focussed was she on her work.

Hours passed and Molina spun, turning the wheel faster now she knew how to work the machine. Basket after basket emptied between her nimble fingers, but she did not stop. She was determined to show the king what her contraption could do in well-trained hands. A week's work in a day, that's what, she told herself, as she lifted the last basket. Her hands ached, but there was so little left, it would be but the work of a moment. And it was — in no time at all, she reached for the door, ready to return to the prince's chamber, only to find the door was locked.

She rapped smartly on the wood. "Captain, I have finished spinning all of the flax!" she called.

She heard the scrape of bolts being drawn, before the door swung open. "Truly?" the captain asked, looking relieved.

He hadn't believed she could do it, Molina realised. Well, she'd proved him wrong, too.

His face fell when he looked around. "But

where is the gold?"

"Gold?" Molina looked blank, then remembered what Lubos had told the king. "The gold comes from selling the extra linen made this way. You can't honestly believe I am a witch who spins flax into gold directly, surely!"

"What I believe matters not. It is the king's command that you remain here until you have spun all the flax into gold thread, as you did yesterday." The captain held up one of yesterday's spindles, still full of the yellow thread that horrid man had touched.

Realisation dawned on her. He hadn't tainted the thread – he'd turned it into gold, thinking it would persuade her to help him. Instead, it had landed her in terrible trouble.

"But I can't…I didn't…" she began, then closed her mouth. She could not tell this guard captain that she'd been visited by a man who wasn't the prince in the prince's very chambers. The man's very presence placed her and her child in danger, for if the king had even the faintest suspicion that the child was not fathered by Lubos, there would be no marriage…instead, she'd be tried for treason. And likely die, along with her unborn child.

"Did you lie to the king yesterday about spinning this thread?" the captain demanded.

"No," she whispered forlornly. "I spun it, with that wheel."

He shoved the golden thread at her. "Then spin the rest like this, and I can return you to the prince's chambers." He left, slamming the door behind him. This time, Molina heard the bolts shoot home, locking her in.

Molina fell to her knees and wept. If the king intended to keep her here until she spun gold from flax, then she would die in this chamber, and never see Lubos again.

Twenty-Six

When the following day came, Abraham had to hunt for the girl. She was not in the tower chamber, nor the bedchamber below it. All day he peeped into rooms all over the sprawling castle, but she had hidden herself well.

It wasn't until after dark that he spotted a light in the maidens' tower that hadn't been there last night. Abraham gazed up at the flickering light, and all the pieces fell into place. She'd been frightened, so she'd taken refuge in the highest, most defensible tower in the middle of the castle. It was heavily guarded, too – she was taking no chances. Guards at the door, in a chamber partway up the tower, and more outside the door to her chamber at the top. If it weren't for his magical shoes, Abraham would have no chance of reaching her.

After making more holes in her tower walls than he'd find in a mountain cheese, finally he emerged in her chamber. Just as before, she was alone with her spinning table toy, and several baskets filled with spindles of spun thread.

The girl herself sat on the floor, weeping.

Abraham hesitated. He had little experience with weeping women, and he did not think this one wanted to be kissed as Maja had.

"I have come for your answer, as I promised," he announced. "Will you help me?"

She raised her red-rimmed eyes. "When you are responsible for all this? Why would I help you?"

Perhaps he hadn't explained himself well enough yesterday. "Because both I and my son will die unless you break the curse that afflicts my family."

"What about me?" she demanded, rising. "I will die because of what you did! If I do not turn all this thread into gold like you did yesterday, the king will have me killed. If you want my help, then fix the mess you have made!"

"You wish me to transform this thread?" Abraham hardly dared to believe it could be so simple.

She glared at him. "The king demands that it be done, after seeing the thread you transformed yesterday."

This must be the danger the seer had spoken of.

"So if I simply turn your thread into gold, you will agree to help me?"

If anything, the fire in her eyes burned even more deadly than before. "If you work your magic on it, then perhaps the king will let me live long enough to consider helping you. For if you do not, he will execute me in the morning."

He would have to save her.

"Very well." Abraham peeled off his gloves, and plunged his bare hands into the nearest basket. Spindle after spindle he touched, until they were all transformed, and then he started on the next one.

Behind him, he heard the girl tip out the basket he'd finished with. Checking his work, no doubt. But she would find no impurities in his gold. Its magical nature required no refinement.

He reached for the third basket.

"You've missed two." She held out the spindles, their pale thread seeming ghostly compared to the shimmering gold of their companions.

Abraham didn't dare risk touching her, especially not without his gloves. "Set them there," he directed, pointing at the wheel table.

"It makes much more sense to do them a few at a time, then place them in the basket once they're done. As I did, when I spun them," she said. "Then you won't miss any."

"I didn't miss any. I just may not have touched them for long enough for the spell to work," Abraham said.

"Well, the second basket had seven you didn't touch. That's ten you've missed. A systematic approach would be much more efficient. Yours isn't the only life depending on this being done right, you know."

Growling, he reached for a fourth basket and dumped the contents on the stone floor. He seized two in each hand, transformed them, then tossed them in the empty basket. "Happy now?"

"I won't be happy until the king releases me, and my husband returns. But at least now I might live another day."

Just as Abraham would not be truly happy until he'd saved his son and could take Maja in his arms again.

"What is this curse someone has cast on you?"

Her question surprised him. Could she not see?

"Someone cast it on one of my ancestors, and it follows his bloodline. So it was passed down to me, and my son. I did nothing to deserve it but be born into the wrong house."

"But what does it do?" she persisted. "You said it will kill you, but..."

"When my death is close, and I have less

than a year to live, everything I touch turns to gold. Unless I wear these gloves." Abraham jerked his chin at the fur lined gloves on the table. "And then one day…or one night, in my father's case…it is over."

She nodded thoughtfully. "So you are given a year to improve your family's fortunes before you die. It does not seem like such a curse to me. All men die, and at least you have more warning than most."

Did she not understand? "We die young. In our prime. Leaving a young wife and child behind, who we cannot touch from the moment the curse takes hold. My family have called it the Touch, for that is the one thing we cannot do. Touch anyone we love. You cannot imagine what it is like!"

"I cannot touch my husband, for the king has sent him on some quest, while he keeps me locked up here. I do not know how long it will be before I can touch him again, or even see him again, for I do not know when he will return. So I know very well what it is like, though my misfortune is the work of men, you and the king, not some mysterious witch casting a curse!"

She was right, curse her, though he didn't dare say it. He set the last golden spindle in the now filled basket. "There. This one is done. On to the next."

She reached for it. "I shall check it first."

He sighed. He could not argue with that, either.

Twenty-Seven

Molina woke up on the floor, surrounded by gold-filled spindles. The strange man was gone, but he'd done his work well. True to his word, he'd turned all the thread into gold. The king would have to be satisfied now.

She rose stiffly and made her way to the door and banged her fist on it. "Captain, I am done," she shouted.

"I will fetch the captain, mistress," came a voice through the door. There was a pause, then a muffled, "It may take some time to find him."

Molina settled down to wait.

By the time she could hear someone unbarring the door, the sun had reached the arrow slits that passed for windows and it streamed down on the artfully piled up spindles, setting the whole room aglow.

The men in the doorway had to shield their eyes against the brightness, so it took them a moment to register her presence. "The king's work is done, Captain, and I would retire to my chamber now," Molina said pointedly.

A man stepped through the door, blinking. The guard captain looked like he'd been woken from a sound sleep.

"I…ah…yes, mistress. Two of my men will see you safely to your chambers. I must…must report this to the king."

Her arms felt leaden after all the spinning she'd done yesterday, so she was relieved when the guardsmen didn't take her arms like they might a prisoner. Instead, they walked behind her, letting her lead the way. As though she truly was Lubos' wife, and not some girl who hoped the king would allow her to marry him. For the madman Lubos had introduced as his father, the king, was not a man she could trust to keep his promises. Unlike his son.

Vowing to hide in Lubos' chambers until he returned, Molina sank into the prince's bed. She had only a moment to wish the prince lay beside her before sleep claimed her for its own.

Twenty-Eight

The following night, Abraham returned to the maiden's tower, where he found the girl sitting at the wheeled table, spinning flax into thread. The walls were stacked with baskets of the stuff, waiting to be spun.

Before he could ask, she said, "The king is not satisfied with what I gave him this morning. He insists I must spin even more. He expects the impossible. No one could spin this much thread in a day, even with a spinning wheel."

"If you merely break the curse, I will leave

you to your work, and never disturb you again," Abraham said.

She slammed her hands on the table and rose. "I know nothing of curses, unless you are one! Even if I can spin the fibres into thread, I cannot turn it into gold, no matter what the king thinks. Only you can do that. I wish you had never come to me at all, for you will surely get me killed!"

"If I help you again, will you break the curse?" Abraham asked.

"Why won't you listen to me? Why won't any of you stupid men listen to me? I do not know how to break curses, spin straw into gold, or work miracles! I understand waterwheels and spinning wheels and mills, but men's minds spin in such strange ways it is a wonder you can survive at all!" A tear trickled down her cheek. "Yet it is my life at stake, because none of you will listen."

Abraham swallowed. The seer had been certain. Only she could break the curse, no one else. For she had been alone in that tower room until he arrived. "Please," he said simply. "I am sorry for whatever trouble I have caused you. If I make amends, if I help you, would you be willing to at least try to help me break the curse?"

She stared at him for a long time before she said, "Once my work is done, maybe I will be of a mind to help you. Though this will take us all night and into the next day, I am certain."

He wanted to shake her, to demand her word, but he could not bring himself to harm the girl. He had less than a year to live, but if she did not do this task the king had set her, he would outlive her. And any hope for his son.

Her wheel whirred into life – she had no time to spare, waiting for his answer when there was work to be done.

Sighing, Abraham set to work.

Twenty-Nine

A night and a day and half the next night it took before Molina finished spinning, as the strange man turned her work from linen to gold. She must have fallen asleep on the spinning wheel, for her back ached from sitting on the stool before it for so long.

The door swung open – the sound of it unbolting must have woken her. The guard captain had returned.

"Get her up. The king wants her moved. Bring the table, too."

"And the stool, sir?"

"All of it."

Molina wished it were a dream, but as two guardsmen took her aching arms, she knew this was worse than any nightmare.

They marched her out of the castle and down the cobbled streets to where she could hear the rushing water of the river. Did they mean to throw her in?

Two men unbarred a massive set of doors, large enough to drive a cart through, which is what someone must have done, for the space she entered stretched for what seemed like miles in the light of the guttering torches. The vaulted ceilings told her she was in some vast storehouse or cellar, filled with baskets of flax.

Distantly, she heard the sound of something being set down on the stone floor. Her spinning wheel and her stool.

"By the king's order, you will stay here and spin, until his warehouse contains nothing but gold," the captain said.

She folded her arms across her chest. "And what if I cannot?"

"Then by the king's command, you shall be put to death." There was pity in the guard captain's eyes. "We all serve the king, mistress, and you must do your duty as I do mine. Set to work, and I will see that a good meal is sent up from the castle kitchens. The crown prince would not want you to starve." He hustled the other guards out, and the heavy bar on the door clanged as it dropped into place.

Molina wanted to cry, but she had no tears left. So she did the only thing she could – sit down and spin, for such was her fate.

Thirty

Day blended into night, for there was no light down here, except that which came from the torches, which guardsmen replaced every day when they brought Molina's meals. The food was not so fine as the fare she'd enjoyed in Lubos' chambers, but it was no worse than some of the things she'd cooked on the nights Helga spent with her family.

Until one morning, when the smell from the stewpot curdled the contents of her belly and she had to bring her dinner back up again.

Too weak to work, she'd lay down on her

straw pallet, pushing the food as far away from her as possible.

If she did not work, she would die down here in the dark, she told herself, but the words were not enough to rouse her. Some illness had laid her low, and she did not know if she would survive it.

Thirty-One

The next night, the girl was not in the crown tower nor the maiden's one, and Abraham despaired of finding her. He searched the castle in vain for three days, until he stumbled across the guard captain carrying a meal out of the castle gates. Curious, he followed the man to the tithe barns by the river, and that was where he found the princess.

Abraham hid in the shadows, waiting for the guard to leave before he stepped inside the barn.

He didn't see her at first, for the place was

stacked with baskets, much like her chamber in the maiden's tower. But what he'd seen in the maiden's tower was a mere millpond compared to the endless sea he saw here.

She sat slumped over her wheeled table, with a half-full spindle beside her. The basket of filled spindles at her feet told Abraham she'd been labouring for the king again, until she fell asleep.

"Princess?" he said, then repeated it, a little louder each time, until he managed to rouse her.

She sat up, blinking. "You," she managed to say before she slumped over the wheel again with a groan. This was more than simple tiredness.

She vomited into a bucket at her feet, then rose unsteadily. "Must…lie down…"

Abraham caught her before she fell. "Are you ill?" he asked, dreading her response. For he might be able to save her from some foe, but illnesses were not something a man could fight with a sword. He laid her gingerly on the pallet she'd been headed toward and backed away.

"Not ill. 'Tis just the baby. The sickness mothers get..." She coughed, and Abraham handed her the bucket just in time.

Maja had been the same, he remembered now. Ill and swearing she was not, until she'd seen the seer and admitted she was carrying his son.

Childbirth could kill a woman in more ways than a sword could. And that was without a king who'd threatened to execute her if she didn't spin straw into gold.

So much for her breaking the curse quickly.

And now he couldn't.

Abraham stared around the barn, and the piled-up baskets of flax. Even if she could break the curse now, it would cost her her life, for without his curse turning the stuff to gold, the king would kill her.

No wonder she didn't consider it a curse.

If he wanted his son to live, he would have to do the work for her. Saving her, and his son.

Abraham sat down on the stool she'd recently vacated, twisting the thread between his gloved fingers as he spun the wheel experimentally. Long ago, Maja had tried to teach him how to spin, but she had not done it with a wheel like this princess did. The thread broke, stuck between his fingers, and Abraham swore.

Too late he remembered the princess was present, but she had fallen asleep and not noticed his foul language. Fortunately.

He tried again, but every time, the thread caught on his gloves and broke. He would have to take them off.

Perhaps it was a good thing the king wanted his thread spun into gold, for between Abraham's bare fingers, the thread glittered as it wound its way around the spinning spindle.

The hours galloped past, but Abraham focussed only on his work. He rested occasionally, making up a second pallet in the shadows at the far end of the barn, where the guards would not see him when they brought the princess her meals.

One day, he woke to find her at the spinning wheel, her nimble fingers working faster than his could, though her slumped shoulders said she did not wish to.

"Let me do that, Princess," he implored.

"You are in no state for such things. Return to your bed and rest."

Her eyes seemed sunken, or perhaps it was a trick of the light. "I will rest when I am dead, which will be soon, if the king has his way. You said once you wished to save your son. Well, I wish I could save my daughter. It seems we will both fail at our respective quests." She stroked her belly wistfully.

That's when it hit him. All the times she'd refused him, told him she could not break the curse. What if it was not the princess, but her daughter? Her daughter would be a princess, too.

"Were you carrying the child when we first met?" he asked eagerly.

"What does it matter to you, bringer of bad fortune? Because of you, she will die when I do."

"Please. I mean you no harm, Princess. Truly. Whatever sins I have committed against you, I pray you will forgive me."

She looked at him long and hard. "I pray I will, too. But not yet. And if it matters, though I have no idea why it might, yes, I was already carrying my husband's child the night you invaded my chamber and made the king think I can work miracles."

Abraham shook his head. "Your husband did that, not I. I was listening when he presented your work to the king. Miracles is his word, not mine. Come with me now, and I will save you from the king and your thoughtless husband, and when your child is born, I will see she is treated like the princess she is."

"I will not leave the man I love. Not for the king, or you, or anyone." She coughed, and reached for the bucket. "Prince Lubos will return. He will help me, and will marry me, just like he promised." She rose shakily to her feet, staggered to her bed, and fell face-first into the straw. After a long moment, she moved so she lay more comfortably. "I must rest. When I wake, I will…work more."

"Swear to me you will give me the child when she is born, and I will spin all the straw in this room into gold," Abraham said. "You will live and stay with your husband, and your sacrifice will save my life and my son's.

The princess coughed again, but she did not reach for the bucket. It took Abraham a moment to realise she was laughing. "Give up my child to you? A strange man I neither know nor trust? You are a fool. No. You shall not have her."

Abraham folded his arms across his chest. "Then I will not help you."

The standoff did not last long. The princess fell asleep, and Abraham went back to work. For he could not let the girl and her daughter die, not if one of them could save his son. And as long as he stayed, he would keep trying to convince her. She would agree eventually. She had to.

Thirty-Two

While the princess slept, he spun. When she awoke, sometimes he would sleep, and at others, he would ask her again. Her answer never changed – she would not give him her child.

Until finally, after several days of being unable to leave her bed as the sickness laid her lower than usual, she said the words he was waiting for: "Yes. If you can spin every bit of flax in this place into gold before the king executes me, then the child is yours."

He wanted to cheer and dance, but

Abraham knew he could not stop working. For while there was work to be done, he could not stop. Because the pain in his chest was increasing, and his days were numbered. If he did not finish his task before the curse claimed him, then this would all be for naught.

Abraham spun until his fingers ached, and then he spun some more. Twisting flax into gold, watching the spool fill, then swapping it for another.

Until he reached for a fresh basket…and found they were all empty. A warehouse full of flax, spun into enough gold to last a kingdom for a century.

He set the last spindle on the pile and searched through the baskets again, but found nothing left to spin.

His work was done.

Abraham rose from his stool, his legs stiff from sitting so long, and staggered over to the wall. He opened a hole in the wall, and made his way back to the cottage where he'd taken up lodgings when he first arrived.

The bed was narrow and hard, little better than the pallet in the warehouse, but he fell facedown on the cool linen, pulled a blanket over himself, and slept the sleep of the dead.

Thirty-Three

Lubos had never ridden so much in his life. He lingered in each barony only long enough to hear the tales of this summer's low harvest and see the truth of it for himself, before heading to the next one. Molina was in his mind, every day and every night. A dozen times a day, he'd turn to see her riding by his side, only to find he rode alone. At night, he'd wake to a bed that was cold and lonely without her. Life was cold and lonely without her.

The faster he fulfilled his quest, the sooner he would stand with her at his side in the new cathedral as his bride.

But the longer he rode, the more he realised his father had sent him on a fool's errand. There were no grounds for his father's suspicions, as he would know if he stepped outside the castle long enough to see the farmlands for himself. Signs of the spring floods were everywhere for anyone with eyes to see. Could his father be so blind in his old age that all he saw were the slights of the past, when what the kingdom needed was a man firmly grounded in the present who could look to the future?

If only his father's body was as unsound as his mind, but Lubos could not recall his father ever knowing a day of ill health. The man might go completely mad, and yet still remain king.

So Lubos filled his saddlebags with written reports about every nobleman he visited, careful to take note of everything he saw, so his father would have no excuse to send him out again. He needed Molina, and he liked to fancy that perhaps she might like to have him home as well.

Or perhaps she was so busy ensuring every woman in the capital owned a spinning wheel and knew how to use it, that she had no thoughts to spare for him at all. Lubos smiled at the thought of a woman who loved machines more than men. At least, most men. He knew she loved him, and that was all that mattered.

When he finally rode across the bridge into the capital, he raised his eyes to the crown tower, where they'd set up her workroom above his bedchamber. Above the bedchamber they shared, he corrected himself, as his body ached to feel hers twined around him once more. Soon, he promised himself, and her, for if she happened to glance out the window, she would surely see him returning.

If only he could go to her first, but his father would want to know the news, and he might withdraw his consent to the marriage if Lubos favoured his bride over king and country. So Lubos trudged wearily to the throne room and made his report, then answered questions until even his father was satisfied.

Afternoon faded into evening before Lubos ascended the steps to the crown tower, and Molina. He'd ordered food to be sent up, for once he entered his chambers, he had no intention of leaving her until the morrow, at least.

He threw open the door, but the chamber was cold, without even a fire to chase out the chill in the autumn air. Strange. Unless Molina had taken to sleeping in her workroom above. Lubos hurried up the stairs, only to find the workroom empty, too. No fire, no spinning wheel, no Molina…where was she?

His father would know, for only his father could order the men of the castle to ignore the crown prince's orders to care for his bride.

Had he sent her home? Forced her to marry that fool, Bachmeier? Or perhaps his half-brother, Xylander? Or worse, had some terrible fate befallen his stepmother, so that the king took Molina for himself? By all that was holy, Lubos prayed this had not happened. For if it had, he would be honour bound to kill his own father, for Molina could not have gone to him willingly.

Lubos broke into a run, headed for the throne room. His father had gone too far now.

The doors to the throne room were closed, and Schuttmann, the captain of the guard, stood in his way.

"Let me pass," Lubos demanded.

Schuttmann shook his head. "You are the heir to the throne. His rages have already driven your brother and sister away. If I let you pass, he will turn his rage on you, and if he orders me to kill you as a traitor, I shall have no choice. The kingdom will need you to take the reins when he is gone. Besides, he has almost forgotten about the girl. If you did not return this week, I would have risked freeing her myself."

"You know where she is?" Freeing her meant she was imprisoned somewhere, not married to someone else. Lubos dared to breathe again. "Take me to her!"

"Yes, Your Highness. She was taken to the maiden's tower, and then to one of the tithing barns."

"Why in heaven's name would she be in a barn? They should be full of..." Too late

Lubos realised there would likely be several empty barns, after this year's poor harvest. But still it did not make sense.

Schuttmann ducked his head. "This one was full of flax, Your Highness. Flax the king commanded her to spin. She has not been harmed, I swear it."

Lubos regarded the guard captain for a long moment. He was a man of honour, who would rather die than be forsworn. A man Lubos would rely on in the future, when Lubos was king. Better to start relying on him now, for the future was coming faster than Lubos liked.

"Take me to her," Lubos repeated, more calmly this time. He followed Schuttmann down to the river, pulling his cloak tighter around him as the evening chill seemed to rise from the very stones beneath his feet.

By the time they'd unbarred and unlocked the doors, it was full dark, and Lubos lit a torch to take inside the pitch-dark barn. A wall of baskets greeted him — empty baskets, which had once contained unspun flax, judging from the fluff clinging to the sides of some of them.

"Molina?" he called, but heard no answer.

He hurried to the end of the makeshift wall, lifting his torch high above his head to illuminate the cavernous space. His breath misted before his face, for he could feel the wintry chill stealing its way through his cloak. The cold was fine for storing food, but this was not the place for Molina.

He stepped deeper into the darkness, until the pool of light from his torch touched something other than stone and baskets. Something that shone back. Golden…balls? Lubos reached down to pick one up, and realised it was not a ball but a spindle, wound around with golden thread. Thousands of them, piled up in a great mountain that stretched nearly to the ceiling.

It would have taken an army of women months to spin so much. Molina could not have done this in the time he'd been gone. Unless she had an army of women, armed with her miraculous spinning wheels…

He rounded the pile, expecting to see the machines, lined up ready for production. But there was only one, sitting in a puddle of light, all alone.

Molina had done this with only one wheel. Working day and night, never ceasing…for how else could she accomplish such a thing? His father had enslaved a free woman. His betrothed.

"Molina?" he called again, louder this time.

The sound he heard was so quiet, he might have imagined it, but Lubos was certain he had not. The smell of damp was stronger here, and there was moss underfoot. He called her name again, and something rustled to his right.

If it was a rat getting his hopes up, he'd skewer it on his sword, Lubos swore, striding forward until he met a pile of mouldy-smelling straw. And amid the straw, a familiar boot. Dropping the torch, he rushed forward to extract the half-buried woman from the straw. Molina's eyes opened slowly, shadowed as though she had not slept for weeks. Then she lifted a thin hand to her lips and coughed hard for what seemed like an eternity.

He waited until the coughing fit subsided before he lifted her in his arms, having to hide his horror at how much lighter she felt. "Were they starving you, my lady?" he choked out.

"I know the castle kitchens regularly sent food, or they did. She hasn't touched this, and it looks two to three days old." Schuttmann nudged a plate with his foot, which sat beside a full jug of water. "The king must have forgotten about her after all."

"Then she can stay forgotten, but I'm taking her home." Lubos wrapped his cloak around her, but he couldn't stop her from shivering. "Summon a physician to my chamber."

"Yes, Your Highness." Schuttmann hurried off into the dark, his torch bobbing as he ran.

Lubos didn't dare run, carrying such a precious burden, but he strode with such purpose not even the gate guards dared to get in his way.

When he reached his chamber, he was pleased to see that someone had lit the fire, and a pot of something warmed on the hearth. He lay Molina on his bed and dared to look at her properly for the first time.

She had not been plump before, but her bones showed through her skin now, and he hadn't imagined the shadows beneath her eyes. He'd seen corpses with more colour, but her laboured breathing told him she still lived.

He peeled off her clothes, worn thin from overuse, and dressed her in one of her new linen shifts before tucking her properly into his bed. Only then did he ladle a bowl of stew from the pot by the fire and bring it to her bedside. He tasted a spoon of the stuff to make sure it wasn't too hot before offering some to her.

"You must be hungry, my lady. You haven't eaten for days. This will help you keep up your strength," he coaxed.

Her eyes fluttered open. "Lubos?" she managed to say before another coughing fit engulfed her.

"The very same," he said lightly, setting the bowl down so that he could support her. "What did they do to you while I was gone? I swear if I had known, I would have come right home." An empty promise, and they both knew it. He could not change the past, no matter how much he wished he could.

"Is he gone?" she asked, peering around.

"Who?" Whoever had frightened her, Lubos intended to see him dead by dawn.

"I do not know his name," she said.

Lubos did not need to know the man's name before he executed him.

"What did he do to you?" he demanded.

She sank back against the pillows. "Nothing. Not yet. But I don't want him to take my child…" Her hands slid down to her belly. Only now did Lubos realise it looked rounder than usual, though she'd lost weight everywhere else.

His fury burned white hot. "This man with no name got you with child?"

Molina smiled wanly. "No, the child is yours. Ours. No man but you has ever touched me like that."

"No other man ever shall," Lubos vowed. "My father said we could marry when I returned. Now I'm home, you shall name the day. As soon as you are well enough to leave my bed, if only for a few hours."

"Your Highness should not have brought some sick girl into your own bed. Heaven knows what diseases she may carry! Send her to the church, where the nuns take care of such charity cases." The physician sniffed.

"And burn all the bedding."

In three strides, Lubos stood before the fool, hauling him up by his collar until his feet dangled above the floor. "Have a care how you speak about the woman I am to marry, for one day she will be queen, and it is your job to make sure she survives. For if she dies, so shall you."

The physician's eyes went wide with terror. Good. "Y-yes, Your Highness," he said.

Lubos dropped him, then pointed to the patient. "Make my wife well again." He stood by the fire, with his arms folded across his chest, and watched.

The physician scurried to Molina's bedside, where her eyes had drifted closed once more. Perhaps it was for the best, as all that poking and prodding could not have been comfortable. Lubos prayed she didn't wake up until the man's examination of her was done, for to see a strange man so close to her would surely terrify what little life she had left out of her.

But Lubos' prayers went unanswered. The moment the physician touched her belly, her hands came up to shield herself. "Don't you take my child!"

The physician muttered something. Lubos only caught two words, but they were enough. He covered the distance between them in a moment, and felt a sense of satisfaction as his fist collided with the insolent man's jaw.

"Call my wife a whore again, or our child a bastard, and they will be the last words you ever utter," Lubos promised him.

The physician rose to his feet, rubbing his jaw. "Are you sure the babe is yours, Your Highness?"

Lubos did not hesitate. "Absolutely. Just as certain as I am when I tell you that if you are responsible for the death of a future queen and the king after me, I will make sure you die a traitor's death."

The physician paled and edged away from Lubos to examine Molina again. He took longer this time, though perhaps that was because he could feel both Molina and Lubos' eyes on him. Finally, he said, "I shall stop by the apothecary's on my way home and ask him to prepare some healing draughts for the girl. I will also give you a list of things a woman in her condition should eat and drink for the best health of the child, so that your castle cook can provide such things. If you should lose her or the child, it is God's will, not mine, for I have done everything I can." He scribbled something down on a roll of parchment and dropped it on the bed. "Your Highness." He bowed and departed.

Molina reached for the paper and unrolled it. "Most of these are just hearty foods. Plenty of meat, and things from the dairy. He left off lamb's lettuce. In the village where I grew up, expectant mothers all had to eat lamb's lettuce every day. To help stave off illness." The paper fell from her fingers and she lay back on the pillow again, paler than before. "I am...so tired, my love. Would you mind if I rest?" She closed her eyes, not waiting for permission.

Lubos smiled. She had been through enough, and she would need plenty of rest in order to recover from whatever she'd endured in his absence. He swore he would make things right, whatever it took.

Thirty-Four

Days passed. Lubos helped Molina to eat a little or take some of the numerous draughts the apothecary sent, though she managed to keep very few of the noxious potions down for very long. Her coughing grew worse, until she barely managed to swallow a thing without coughing it back up again. Lubos despaired as she seemed to grow even thinner before his eyes.

Hourly, he sent orders to the castle kitchens for the nourishing foods on the physician's list, but nothing could nourish her if it didn't make it down her throat.

The only thing the cook did not send up was lamb's lettuce, for the cook claimed to know nothing of a food by that name.

Lubos wanted to weep, or break something, or tear his own hair out by the roots. He was being forced to watch the woman he loved die, and there was nothing he could do about it.

Captain Schuttmann made the mistake of visiting and Lubos almost pitched him out the door again. Almost, but some spark of reason far in the back of his mind reminded him that without Schuttmann, he would never have found her, so Lubos sank back on his chair and simply stared balefully at the guard captain instead.

"How is she?" Schuttmann asked.

Lubos waved his hand at the bed. "See for yourself."

Schuttmann's expression said it all. "I am sorry we were too late to help her. I came to tell you that the king has given you permission to marry the girl, now she has spun to his satisfaction."

Lubos wasn't sure whether he wanted to

laugh or cry. "She can't keep her eyes open long enough to speak the vows, and as long as she cannot eat anything without bringing it back up again, she cannot gain any strength. And to make matters worse, she's carrying our child!"

Schuttmann's eyebrows rose. "She is with child? My wife had terrible morning sickness with our first child. Couldn't eat a thing for weeks, and she didn't have the strength to leave her bed, either. I ate in your father's hall most nights, for she could not cook. When she carried our second child, she caught a chill, much like your girl here, and I thought I'd lose them both, but there's a witch who lives over on the south side of the mountain, and she has medicinal plants that grow nowhere else but her garden. I paid a fortune for some leaves from a plant called a rapunzel, which she said would help my wife to fight the illness. Watching my wife eat leaves like a rabbit, I thought it a foolish notion, until she began to improve. They say physicians and priests and prayer are all we should need for health, but sometimes we need to go back to the old ways, and the old gods, for witches know things that priests and physicians would never dream about."

Lubos stared at his sleeping lady. The lady who might never wake again. "Can you get this miraculous plant for me? I dare not leave her. Any moment might be her last."

Schuttmann shook his head. "Nay, that I cannot. Witches have their ways, and I dare not cross one. Whether a king or a commoner, if you want something from a witch, you must ask her yourself. It's half a day's ride – if you leave now, and ride through the night, you might be back in time to feed your lady leaves to break her fast on the morrow."

And if he did not, and she died during the night, he would never forgive himself. Lubos planted a kiss on her fevered brow, praying it would not be the last, and headed out of the room, towards the stables. He would find the witch, persuade her to part with the plant, and return on the morrow to save Molina. And when she recovered, he would marry her, like he'd promised.

Thirty-Five

Darkness had fallen by the time he arrived at the walls around the witch's garden. This had to be the place, for the rest of the mountain was covered in vineyards and these stone walls looked positively ancient. There was just one problem: the gates were closed, and no matter how loudly Lubos knocked or shouted, no one came to open them.

All his frustration and fury at losing Molina bubbled up. He'd ridden so far, willing to do anything to save her, and the witch wasn't about to let the crown prince of the realm she lived in through the gates?

To hell with that.

Lubos found a spot where the wall looked easier to climb, and started up. It had been some time since he'd climbed anything, but it was a skill, once learned, that a man never forgot. A handhold here, a toehold there, stretching for a new one, one limb at a time, until he could haul himself over the top of the wall.

From the surprisingly wide top, he had his pick of trees to climb down to reach the ground below. The garden stretched out as far as a vineyard in the moonlight, carved up into beds by myriad paths that went everywhere. It was a labyrinth with a thousand ways through to your destination – much like the capital, but with patches of plants where the buildings should be.

Each plot had a little post with a sign on top, that was surprisingly easy to read in the moonlight. It must be some sort of magic, Lubos realised, glancing around. What other spells lurked within these walls?

He was so intent on finding the sign with

rapunzel on it that he nearly missed the right plot, for the sign said lamb's lettuce. He snorted to himself. Molina was correct, as usual. He peered at the sign again, and was surprised to see that it had changed so that it clearly said rapunzel. Magic for sure. Lubos shivered.

Well, whether it was rapunzel or lamb's lettuce, this was what he needed. He stooped to pick a handful, and the whole plant came up, like a turnip. He shook the soil free, then opened a sack and slipped the plant inside. He stared at the remaining plants for a long moment, debating whether he dared take more. For if one was not enough…he would not have time to ride back here for more.

In the end, he took three, reasoning that if one had been enough for Schuttmann's sick wife, then he would need at least two for Molina. Three…just in case.

He'd brought a bag of gold coins to trade for the plants, and he emptied the pouch into one of the holes he'd left, as payment. Though he'd climbed the wall at night and taken the plants without asking the owner, he was a prince and a man of honour, not a thief. That much gold would feed a family for a year. More than enough payment for three plants.

Tying the sack shut, he flung it over his shoulder. Now he had another decision to make: back over the wall, the way he'd come, or through the gate, which surely opened from the inside?

Leaving the gate open would surely alert the witch that she'd had a visitor, but Lubos had never intended his visit to be a secret. She'd know once she reached the rapunzel beds, regardless.

He strode confidently toward the gate, holding tight to his precious sack of plants.

Only to find a figure stood in his way.

The witch lifted her lantern. "Who dares steal from Mistress Kun?"

Lubos swallowed. "I am Crown Prince Lubos, heir to the king, and I have left fair payment for the plants I took. Let me pass, for a woman's life depends on them."

The witch did not budge. "I decide what is a fair price, not you." Her eyes seemed to glow blue in the darkness. "What is it you have taken? Ah, the rapunzel. You lie, Prince. More than one life depends on the plants you hold."

Lubos hung his head. "'Tis true. The woman I love is carrying our child. We were betrothed to be married, but she has fallen ill, and I fear for her life." He paused, then added, "And for the child."

"What is this woman's life worth to you?" the witch demanded.

"She is worth more to me than everything I own, including my own life," Lubos said without hesitation.

"What would you give me, if I let you leave with your pilfered plants, and my solemn promise to you that both the woman and her child will live long and healthy lives?"

For Molina? "Anything," he said.

The witch smiled and named a terrible price.

Thirty-Six

"That's the last of the lamb's lettuce. I hope it is enough, for we have no more," Lubos said. He sounded...cheerful.

Molina struggled to open her eyes. They felt as heavy as the rest of her, as though they had not moved in far too long. Her hand flew to her belly, checking that it still swelled with the child growing inside her. She lived, and Lubos was home. She blinked against the bright morning light, and came face to face with a plate of leaves.

Lamb's lettuce, her mind supplied. She'd

never liked it in the past, but now she had the most irresistible craving to devour every last leaf. She reached for it.

"It worked!" Large, warm hands seized hers, and a man's bearded face loomed alarmingly close for a moment until she recognised Lubos beneath the scrubby beard. Then he kissed her.

She batted him away weakly. "It scratches," she complained.

"I'll shave immediately," he promised, then stopped. "Though I should feed you first."

Molina waved her hand. "I can manage these leaves. You…get rid of that horrible hedge."

He laughed and bowed low. "As my lady commands."

She'd almost finished her salad by the time a servant came with warm water and soap, so Molina sat back and watched Lubos shave in the bronze mirror by the window. Her heart soared to see him again. All the darkness…all that drudgery…but that was done now. It must be, for she was back in his chambers, just as the guard captain had promised.

"Molina, can you tell me what happened?

Why you were in that barn full of baskets and balls?" Lubos' eyes gazed at her from his reflection.

She swallowed. She could lie and say she did not remember, but she was no coward. She could not shrink from the truth, especially when Lubos asked for it.

So she told him about the tower room, and the barn, and the spindle he'd given his father that inspired the king's commands. To her surprise, even as she told him about her exhaustion, the pain in her hands from working all hours, and every hardship she had endured, the weight on her shoulders seemed to lessen. Almost as if her ordeal no longer had the power to hurt her.

When Lubos sat beside her on the bed and pulled her into his arms, she did not resist. She'd craved his embrace for longer than she'd wanted those leaves, and she loved him. Loved him with all her heart and soul. And when her body had healed, she'd love him again with that, too.

If he forgave her for what she'd done.

Reluctantly, she pulled away from him.

"There is more. The spindle you gave your father wasn't ordinary thread. It was gold thread, pure gold."

"That's not possible," Lubos said. "No one can spin flax into gold. You told me that. Gold comes from selling the linen…"

Oh, how his thoughts mirrored what her own had been. But no more. "Without magic, yes. But there was a man. That first day I managed to get the spinning wheel working, he came into my workroom. Just walked in, and I first thought he was you. He…he begged to me to break some curse, saying I was the only one who could, and some seer had told him so. He begged me to come with him to do it, and I refused. He offered me all the wealth I would ever need, so I would never need to spin again, and placed his hands on my spindle. The one you took to your father. And then he heard you coming, and he walked through the floor, just as you came in. I barely believed my own eyes, for how could a man walk through solid stone without magic?"

Lubos nodded. "You seemed…agitated, but you told me you were excited at having the wheel working."

"It was true. I was excited. And then he came in, said nonsensical things, and left. I thought perhaps I had gone mad, and did not wish you to know you had promised to marry a madwoman, so I did not tell you. Not that you gave me much time. You were so excited, you grabbed the spindles off my wheel and took them to your father. All filled with gold thread."

Molina took a deep breath. "I did not notice it was gold. Neither did you, I assume. But your father did, and after you left…he had the guard captain take me to a room filled with flax, and he told me to spin. I did, spinning until my fingers cramped and I could scarcely see straight, until every spindle was full of fine linen thread. I'd worked a miracle – doing a week's work in a day, but it was not enough for the king. He had a spindle of gold thread, and my work wasn't done until I'd spun it all into gold."

Lubos gritted his teeth. "My father will rot in hell for this, I swear it!"

Molina hushed him. What happened to the

king after his death was no business of hers, and the same fate might await her, too, for what she'd done. And she still hadn't told Lubos yet. "The strange man appeared, walking through the locked door as though it wasn't even there. He asked me if I'd thought about his offer, and I…I lied, told him I was still considering it, but I would be able to think better once he'd turned the thread to gold, just like he had the other one the day before. All he had to do was touch the thread, and it turned to gold. It was…magic, truly. I was allowed to return to your chamber to sleep, but the next day, I was marched to the tower room again, and forced to spin again. Once more, the man appeared, and begged me to break his curse, which was to turn all he touched into gold, but I told him I could not until he had turned all the flax, too."

A sob caught in her throat, and Molina took a moment to wipe away her tears before she could continue.

"The next morning, the guard captain took me across town, down to the big warehouses by the river. It was full of flax – more than I could spin in a year, without the spinning wheel. I protested that no one could complete this task, and the captain told me the king's command was that I had two choices. I could spin this flax into gold, and when I was finished, I would be allowed to marry his son. Or I could refuse, and I would be executed for daring to disobey the king." She swallowed. "I had no choice, so I sat down and spun. It was not so bad at first, for some of the flax was poorly combed, and not suitable for spinning. Enough to make a bed for me on the first night, and one of the guards brought me food and drink. But one day the food did not smell quite right, and some strange sickness seemed to stop me from rising from my bed. I could not…could not keep food down, nor water. This went on for some days, until I was too weak to move. I think I slept, but I do not know. I awoke to find the strange man kneeling beside me, coaxing me to eat. For I had to break his curse, he said, and I could not break it unless I lived."

Lubos held out his arms. "I am so sorry, my lady. I should have been here, to defend you from strange men and from my father."

Molina shook her head, refusing the comfort he offered. He did not know everything yet. "He fed me, and he did my work for me, spinning that flax into golden thread. He wore gloves when he fed me, but when he spun, he took them off. It was the touch of his bare hands that turned things to gold. I saw it happen with my own eyes so many times, I could not doubt it. And then in the middle of it all, he demanded I repay him for his hard work, and break the curse. I was forced to admit that I was not a witch, and I did not know how to break a curse, but I told him it was his cursed hands that had landed me in this mess, and if he did not spin all the flax into gold like that first spindle, then his hands would be triply cursed with my blood, and that of my unborn child."

Now she wept freely, for she knew she would lose Lubos when he learned what she had done.

"When I told him about our child, his anger faded, like clouds after a storm. He muttered something about how it must be the child, not me. And he refused to finish the work he'd started, unless I promised to give him the child. Our baby. He swore he would care for her as though she was his own daughter, in a castle just as grand as this, but if I did not, then I was cursing him and his son to death, and my death, and that of my daughter, would be on my head, and not his."

Lubos closed his eyes. "You accepted his offer, and promised him the child."

Molina nodded, tears coursing down her cheeks, as words deserted her.

"Curse my father to hell for forcing you to make such a terrible choice. I wish I could thank your stranger for helping you when I could not, but perhaps there is time for that yet, for he will come to take the child when the baby is born, will he not?" Lubos asked. He seemed far too calm. He should be cursing her, not accepting this. She had given away their child to save her own worthless life.

Lubos pulled her into his arms, and kissed the top of her head. "Do not worry about it. Rest, recover, and think only of our wedding, which will be as soon as you are strong enough to leave this bed. When the man returns, I will defend you, and the baby. He shall not take the child from you, I swear."

Molina sniffled and stared up into his eyes. Lubos was a man of honour, who did not break his oaths. For him to swear such a thing… "You are too good for me," she whispered.

Lubos did not reply, but he leaned down to kiss her, wrapping her arms more tightly around her, and for that moment, she forgot everything but the love they shared.

Thirty-Seven

A baby's cry roused Abraham from a sound sleep. "Has your time come already?" he mumbled, forcing his eyes open.

But the eyes he met were not those of the princess. They were accusing, and they belonged to Chase.

"Why aren't you protecting Maja?" Abraham grumbled, rising.

"Because her time came early. She stumbled on the steps and fell. She bled so much, it was a miracle they managed to save the baby. Isaak, she called him. The son you do not deserve."

Chase pointed.

Abraham's gaze followed the direction of his brother in law's finger, to where a strange woman held a baby to her breast. "Maja?" It couldn't be.

"Maja is dead. Giving birth sapped what little life she had left, but she was adamant that the child must live. That you might love him as you never loved her." Chase's fist slammed into the table. "Tell me you have succeeded in your quest. That my sister did not die to give you a son you will kill through carelessness."

Abraham hung his head. "I have not broken the curse yet. I do not know for certain which princess —" He stopped as realisation dawned. The girl he'd found spinning was not a princess, for she had yet to marry the prince. But the child she carried... "The princess has not been born yet," he breathed, so softly he wasn't sure Chase heard.

Chase made an exasperated sound. "You have pinned your hopes on a princess and a witch? You are an even bigger fool than I thought."

"The girl's mother has promised to give the

child to me the moment she is born. She will –
"

"You have a child! Your son! You need to care for him, not some royal bastard you have stolen!" Chase roared.

"You must…engage a wet nurse. She can care for the boy. While we watch and wait for the princess to give birth. I mean…the lady. The prince's bride. And the baby will…."

"Wail and cry and be of little use, as all babies are until they grow up! You truly have lost your wits."

Abraham stared at his brother in law. "The princess will save my son. She is the only one who can. Have faith, my friend, and all will be revealed in time." He wanted to believe his own words, but for the first time, he feared he would not live to see his prediction come true. For the princess might be the only one who could break the curse…but it might be many years before she could. Years he did not have.

"We will watch and wait," Abraham said with finality. What more could he do?

Thirty-Eight

Molina woke slowly, revelling in the feeling of Lubos' warm body pressed against her back as he reached around her to cup her breasts. "More, my lady wife?" he whispered in her ear.

"Of course," she murmured back, sighing with pleasure as he eased into her from behind. Her belly was too big now for the frenzied lovemaking of their first nights together, or even on their wedding night, but still he'd found a way to fulfil his promise of making love to her every night, and every morning, too. His hands knew her body so well he soon had her gasping, then crying out his name, as the first wave of pleasure crashed over her. As ever, he waited for the third time before his shout for joy drowned out hers. An amazing lover and a loving husband – Molina could not ask for more.

He withdrew from her and helped her wash, before cleaning himself up, too. Lubos set a fresh log on the fire, warming the wintry room so that she would not take another chill. Then he crept back into bed and stroked her belly, eliciting an angry kick from the child inside.

"Do you think he will come today?" he asked.

"I hope she will," Molina replied, as she always did.

Lubos laughed then, and rose to dress for the day. He might be the crown prince and not the king, but the king's mind was definitely slipping, and more and more duties fell to Lubos now, for no one wanted to risk his head by going to the king with anything the king might consider bad news. And there was no rhyme or reason for the things he decided constituted bad news. Why, the courier who had brought word of Lubos' younger sister, Guinevere's marriage to a neighbouring king was accused of lying and hanged for his supposed crime, despite bearing a scroll that bore both Guinevere and her husband's seal, for the king had no memory of agreeing to such a marriage.

"Bar the door, until I knock," Lubos warned her as he left. Molina rose to do as he commanded, for that was the only way to protect her from the king, and the guards who were still loyal to him. The only times she opened the door were to allow a maid inside to bring her meals, or to let Lubos back in once his day was done.

Thirty-Nine

Small pains had bothered her for days now, but when her contractions truly started, Molina knew without a doubt that her baby was coming. She seized the bell rope and yanked on it, hearing the jangle of alarm bells summoning the servant who stood watch outside her room, ready to bring the midwife. She heard the patter of running feet as another contraction gripped her, leaving her gasping.

When the pain had eased, Molina turned her attention to the door. She needed to unbar it to let the midwife in. It took her two tries before she managed to heft the bar from its brackets, and a third to tip it onto the floor so that the door could open. Then another contraction seized her, and she fell to her knees.

For a long moment, she knew nothing but pain, and then, she was free. She staggered to her feet, headed for the bed.

"Molina? My lady, are you all right?" Lubos' voice had never sounded so heavenly as it did right now.

She fell heavily into bed, landing on her side so she didn't hurt the baby. "No. Your baby is determined to escape today."

The door flew open, and his eyes shone as bright and eager as the morning sun. "It is time?"

Molina attempted to nod, but all she could manage was a grimace as the pain came again.

Huge hands gripped hers, strong and reassuring. "The midwife is coming, and I have told the physician to stay away on pain of death. What do you wish me to do?"

Molina managed a smile. "Have the baby for me?"

"If I could take the pain from you, I would, but only a woman can bear a child. Men were not made for such things, I fear. But seeing as you will do all the hard work, you must name him. I hope you have some suitable names for a future king picked out."

"Daughter," she bit out before crying out in pain.

When she opened her eyes again, the midwife was there, accompanied by several maids carrying armloads of linen and buckets of water.

"Time to go, for this is no place for men," the midwife said, attempting to shoo Lubos from the room.

As Lubos' hand slipped from hers, Molina only gripped it tighter. The strange man's words came to Molina again, reminding her that she might not live to see or name her child.

She waited for the next pain to pass, before gasping out, "What if I do not survive the birth? Many women die. What if this is the last time I ever see you?"

Lubos leaned down to kiss her forehead,

lowering his voice so only Molina could hear him. "I swear to you, both you and the child will survive. When you were ill and I feared you would not live another night, I went to a witch for your lamb's lettuce. She bespelled the leaves, promising you and the child a long and healthy life. So worry not. Today is not your time."

A witch? For such a powerful spell, she would have exacted a terrible price. All the gold in the tithing barn, perhaps, though witches were not known for their fondness for gold. No, her price would be far higher.

"What did it cost..." she began, before another cry of pain was all she could utter.

Lubos bowed, blew a kiss to her, and departed.

And Molina descended into what could only be described as hell, a realm of pain and pushing and panting that went on for an eternity, until she heard a lusty wail that had not come from her own throat.

"She's perfect, the little princess," someone said.

Molina felt a surge of triumph. She was

right, and the baby was a girl.

Forty

"Sir? The midwife has been called up to the castle."

Abraham blinked. He couldn't have slept away half the day, could he? He just felt so tired all the time, and the pain in his chest was constant now. He didn't have long left. So to lose a day to sleep…

"You promised a copper coin, sir, if I brought you news," the small boy reminded him.

Abraham fished in his pocket and pulled out a silver coin. "Thank you. Now, go back to the midwife's house and tell me when she returns, and I will turn that coin into a gold one."

The boy's eyes grew round. "Truly?"

Abraham nodded gravely. "Truly."

The boy raced back toward the city.

Childbirth took a long time, or so Abraham believed, so he would have time to take the pain draught he'd bought from the apothecary before he had to head into the castle to claim the child. The stuff was terribly bitter, so it was best drunk mixed with wine, and he would need a clear head when he confronted the princess, for the girl had married her prince now.

He poured the powder into a cup, then waited for the wine to warm over the fire. He'd thought his castle was cold, but it had nothing on this cottage. Even with the fire blazing, the tips of his fingers were blue.

When steam curled up from the pot, he poured the wine into his cup, stirring it with his finger until the bitter medicine dissolved. Then he drank it down and lay back against the wall. He could hear the thump of Chase's arrows hitting the target in rapid succession.

His brother in law had always been an expert marksman. Why, he could shoot the very flies from the air. He hoped Chase would teach Isaak to shoot, when the boy was old enough to draw a bow.

Despite his best efforts to stay awake, Abraham drifted off into sleep again.

Forty-One

"The princess has given birth to a beautiful baby girl," the midwife said, rousing Lubos from his doze. He wasn't sure what day it was, or when he'd chosen to lay down to sleep on the cathedral floor, before the very altar, but he had enough sense to know he should get up before one of the priests discovered him and kicked him out of the house of God.

"Is she well?" he asked, scrambling to his feet. Despite his words to Molina, he still didn't trust the witch. Not when he had yet to pay her price. If she chose not to honour their bargain…

"Princess Molina is very tired, for she has been in labour a day and a night, but once she has rested, she should be well. It was an easy birth."

The cries she'd uttered said otherwise, but Lubos did not correct the midwife. Molina would tell him the truth of it, and whether she wanted the same midwife again next time. For there would be a next time. There had to be, for he would need an heir.

"Can I see her?" he asked timidly. It had been a long time since he'd asked anyone for anything, but the realm of women and babies was new to him. He didn't want to do something wrong.

"She is sleeping, and should not be disturbed," the midwife said.

His heart sank, but only for a moment, as he realised she hadn't actually refused him. Could a midwife give orders to the crown prince?

He rose to his full height, hoping he could manage to look regal despite not having shaved after sleeping on the floor. "I must see her, and the child."

The midwife sighed. "Yes, Your Highness. But for only a moment."

Lubos had not run through the castle so fast since he was a boy. He startled several servants, but today he did not care. He was a father, and Molina lived.

He found her tucked up in his bed, amid layers of fresh linen. The faint smell of blood lingered, but a maid brought in a fresh basket of rushes and proceeded to lay them on the floor, and then he could smell only the aroma of summer hay, as out of place in the heart of winter as he was in the women's domain this room had been, only hours earlier.

The cradle moved, just the tiniest bit, though no hand or breeze had touched it. Lubos held his breath and approached.

The baby's eyes were closed, her head crowned with an abundance of dark curls. She lifted a tiny fist from the blankets and waved it in the air, as if cursing something in her dream, before lowering it again.

"So tiny. So perfect," he breathed.

"Isn't she?"

Lubos started. Molina's eyes were open, and

she wore a tired smile. Yet her expression glowed with happiness.

"I wished for a girl," she said softly. "But you must protect her. Swear to me that you will not let the strange man have her. You must take her away, hide her from him, and stand guard over her, until I tell you it is safe. Please, Lubos."

The words came easily. "I swear no strange man shall steal her from you."

"Take her. Take her now, for surely the whole kingdom knows about the birth, and he will come for her soon." Molina reached into the cradle and scooped out the little bundle, no larger than a loaf of bread. A tiny person. "Take her!"

Still Lubos hesitated as the baby was thrust into his arms. "I'm afraid I will drop her," he admitted. "She's so tiny."

Molina's eyes burned with determination, despite the dark circles framing them. "You are her father, and you will neither drop her nor allow her to come to harm. You swore an oath, Lubos, and you will not break it."

He held the child tightly, his heart sinking.

Yes, he had sworn many oaths, and he would break none of them. Even if it broke his own heart to do so.

"She will be safe," he promised himself as much as Molina. He had to believe it.

Forty-Two

Every hoofbeat felt like a nail hammered into his own coffin, but still Lubos rode on. He had sworn he would give anything in exchange for Molina's life, and he could not lose her now.

The massive stone walls rose up sooner than before, or so it seemed. The gates swung open for him today, though he saw no one who might have pushed them. Magic, he told himself, and shivered. This made the child squirm against his chest, as though she felt his fear. Lubos wrapped a protective arm around her, though the swaddling wraps bound her securely to him. He would fulfil his oaths to Molina and to the witch, for he was a man of his word. Even if Molina hated him for it when she found out.

"Enter, Your Highness," the witch called, emerging from a tiny cottage Lubos had not seen nestled under four huge trees. A sacred grove from ancient times, his brain supplied, and he shivered again.

He stepped forward, refusing to give in to his fear. He was a prince, and not a coward. "I come to fulfil the bargain we made. You promised that my wife and child will live long and healthy lives."

She seemed younger than the first time he'd seen her, barely more than a girl, but her eyes glittered with the same ancient secrets he'd glimpsed on his first visit. "And they will. Your queen will outlive you, and hold her son's heir in her arms when your son takes the throne."

Lubos let out a breath he hadn't known he'd been holding. "And the child? Our daughter?"

The witch grinned. "The little weaver. I have waited a long time for this moment." She held out her arms. "Give her to me."

Lubos crossed his arms over his chest. "Not until you swear to me she will be treated like the princess she is, and cared for as well as her mother might."

The witch laughed. "Princesses are raised to be pawns in a much larger game, married off at the convenience of their fathers to cement this or that alliance. Much like your sister Guinevere, married to a man she does not love. Your daughter will be much more than a bedwarmer and broodmare for one of your allies. She will shape the future of many kingdoms, like one of the ancient queens of legend. I will take her to a place so safe, no one will ever find her to steal or harm her. She will outlive her mother, though she will not bring any kings into the world."

"I will have your word." Lubos would not give her the child without it.

"Yes, you are a man of words, when there is so much more to the world. Yet you shall have mine. I swear upon my own life that I will do everything in my power to prolong her life and health. No other girl child will be as precious to her mother as your child will be to me."

Lubos wanted to trust her, if only because she promised so much of what he wanted. Yet even as he untied the baby from her bindings, taking her weight in his arms for what might be the last time, he did not want to surrender her.

"Give her to me!" the witch demanded, her eyes glowing blue.

Unwillingly, Lubos held out the child.

It took only a moment, and his arms were empty. The next moment, he blinked and both the witch and the baby were gone, leaving him alone in the garden.

Tears streamed down his cheeks, and Lubos longed to throw himself to the ground and weep, but he dared not. He had done what he had to, and there was more to come.

He had to tell Molina that in order to keep the girl safe, she could never see her daughter again. So he forced himself back on his horse, and it felt like every hoofbeat landed on his chest, breaking through his ribs and crushing his heart beneath them.

Molina would never forgive him for such a betrayal.

Forty-Three

Abraham took the stairs slowly, but he was still out of breath when he reached the top, so he took his time to recover before he entered the princess's chamber. When he no longer felt dizzy, he tried the door, which opened at a touch.

He stepped inside, then stopped to survey the sleeping girl in the bed. Only her face was visible, but it was no longer skeleton pale, like he remembered it. The dark circles were there beneath her eyes, but she'd been in labour for a day or more, so the sleeplessness was to be expected.

How he could have believed she was a witch, capable of breaking the curse…he had taken the seer's words too seriously, and it was not his fault he'd mistaken her for the princess she would become. A capable woman whose courage knew no bounds. Yet she was not a witch, but an ordinary woman. Her husband was a lucky man.

But a man who would have to beget another daughter, for his firstborn was promised to Abraham. Abraham took a deep breath, and crept deeper into the room. To the cradle that stood beside the princess's bed, within easy reach. All he had to do was reach in, take the child, and leave, but he could not bring himself to steal her.

The princess had gone through so much…she deserved to know the truth, all of it, about why he needed her daughter. And…where the child would be, and that the girl would be safe. For she was no friend of the king's, and if the princess ever needed a place to shelter from the king's wrath, then his home was open to her.

And perhaps she wanted to say farewell to her daughter. Abraham owed the young mother that much.

He slid his gloved hands into the cradle, intending to pull out the child with all her blankets to insulate her from the cold, but the blankets were empty. The child was not here.

Abraham closed his eyes. He had failed. Failed himself, and failed his son. All those days and nights spinning straw into gold to placate a mad king…wasted. He might as well have stayed home with Maja.

"She is gone where you cannot reach her," the princess said.

Abraham's eyes snapped open, to meet her gaze. "You promised her to me. She is the only one who can save my son. I spun you a king's ransom in gold, ten times over, so that you would help me. Faithless woman!"

Her eyes widened and he realised he'd raised a hand to strike her. He lowered it quickly. He had never struck a woman, and he had no intention of doing so now. She could live with the shame of breaking her oath.

"I am Sir Abraham von Rumpelstiltskin, and

my son Isaak will be the last of my line, because of you. Many years ago, my ancestor was cursed with the Touch, and he passed it down, father to son, until it came to me. I know not what my ancestor's crime was, but I have done nothing to deserve this fate. My son is but a baby – a few weeks older than your own daughter – and he is innocent. He does not deserve to die young, and see everything he touches turn to cold metal. I beg you, Princess, have pity on a father who only wishes to save his son." Abraham fell to his knees in supplication.

Tears trickled down the princess's cheeks as she shook her head. "I am sorry, Sir Abraham, but I cannot. My husband has taken her I know not where, and he will defend her with his life. I could never save you or your son, no matter how much I wish I could. I am merely Molina, a miller's daughter from a barony far to the south of here, with no special powers and no title until the prince married me. My only skill is with a spinning wheel. If I could spin a wheel and change your fate, I would, but fate is a weaver and I have no skill in that. I thank you for everything you have done for me. If not for you, both my daughter and I would be dead at the king's hand. I only wish I could return the favour."

"Then we are lost." He rose to his feet, waiting until the light-headedness faded, before heading for the door. He had pinned all his hopes on the princess, and she had dashed them in one blow.

"What are you doing in my son's bed, slut? And who is this vagabond? Is his chamber your whorehouse now?"

Abraham lifted his eyes from the flagstone floor to meet the gaze of an angry old man. An old man wearing a robe woven from gold thread.

The mad king. If it had not been for him, Molina would have told Abraham the truth long ago, and neither of them would have spent the summer locked in a barn, spinning their fingers raw.

If not for this man, Abraham might have had the time to find a way to save his son.

"Get out. Both of you!" the king snapped. "Guards!"

Abraham pulled off his gloves. "Are you the one who wanted straw turned into gold?"

The king looked smug. "I have all the gold I need. We are now the richest kingdom on the continent. But if I need more, my son's wife will provide. Which is why this slut will get out of his bed, for that is where his wife should lie, while he begets an heir on her!"

The mad king did not even recognise his son's bride. The girl who had almost died for his greed. As Isaak would die for it.

Abraham let his fury rise up, his blood heating to boiling until it felt like molten gold in his veins. Perhaps it was.

"The princess will spin no more for you. Take your gold, and I hope it makes you happy in hell!" Abraham laid his hands on either side of the king's face, and the king began to scream. The sound still rang in Abraham's ears, long after it had stopped, and he opened his eyes to view his handiwork. The king was surely the ugliest statue Abraham had ever seen, and that was with his clothes on. Abraham touched the king's robe and boots, until they, too, were solid gold.

He turned to find the princess standing on the bed, backed up against the wall, her eyes wide with terror. "You…you killed the king!" she breathed.

"He deserved to die," Abraham said simply. "My son will be avenged."

He heard the clatter of running feet on the stairs. The guards the king had summoned, he guessed. Abraham knew he had little time left, and he had no intention of spending it in a prison cell in this castle for killing the king.

Abraham stamped on the floor three times, then touched the spot with the toe of his shoe. The flagstones opened up, and swallowed him.

Forty-Four

Lubos had hoped to find Molina asleep, but she sat up the moment he entered their chamber. "Where is Tessarina?" she demanded.

"Who?" he asked. Grief and a long day's ride had surely addled his wits.

"Our daughter," she said. "You said I might name her, and I thought…"

"It's a lovely name," Lubos soothed her.

"But where is she?"

Lubos swallowed. This was the part he'd dreaded most. "She is with the witch who saved your life when you were so sick. She swore she would protect her, keep her safe, and treat her better than any princess. A witch who can defeat death itself will protect her far better than you or I could, especially against a man who can walk through walls and turn things to gold at a touch. When your strange man comes – "

She cut him off. "He has come and gone, stamping a hole in the floor through which he vanished. I have never seen anything like it. I know not where he has gone, but I hope he never returns. When I told him he could not have her, he flew into such a temper, I was certain he would kill me." She smiled wanly. "But instead, he saved me from your father."

Lubos did not believe what he was hearing. "My father? The king?"

"The late king. Abraham von Rumpelstiltskin killed him." Molina pointed at the door. No, at a statue by the door.

Lubos swallowed. The man had turned his father into a statue? He didn't want to get closer, but he had to be sure.

The statue appeared to be a perfect replica

of his father in one of his most violent rages. Bulging eyes, mouth wide open as he spat vitriol based on the delusions of his own mad mind, with his finger pointed at the long-gone target of his rage. Not the way he would want to be remembered, and definitely not the way Lubos wanted to remember him, yet here he was. It looked like Molina's strange man had encased his skin in bronze. No, gold, like the thread he'd helped her spin.

"Is he truly made of gold? We should try to get him out of it, to see if he still lives," Lubos said. But how did one extract a man from his own gold skin?

Molina shook her head. "He is solid gold right the way through, and much too heavy to move. Just as the thread von Rumpelstiltskin spun was pure gold."

Rumpelstiltskin? He had heard of such a place. A barony he'd visited, surely. Lubos racked his brain, searching for the memory. A castle on an island, in the river close to the western borders, protecting the richest trade routes to the west. Its owner was a wealthy man, one of the few who had turned in his regular tithe this year, the last man likely to be making a nuisance of himself here in the capital. Even his father had no quarrel with the man or his ancestors, loyal since the days of Charlemagne.

Well, he'd had no quarrel before. If he'd still lived, Father might not be so peaceable toward the family now. Now it would fall to Lubos to exact justice for regicide. To think Molina had been alone with the man…he should have been here, protecting her, instead of riding around the countryside meeting with witches.

He cupped Molina's face in his hands and pressed his forehead to hers. "My queen, can you ever forgive me?"

She blinked several times in surprise, before she responded, "My king, there is nothing to forgive. If you swear our daughter is safe, then I must trust you. I will miss her, but she will never be safe here while von Rumpelstiltskin lives. You must do as you think best. Such is the burden of a crown."

A crown. Thank the heavens his father had not been wearing it when he entered Molina's chamber. "A burden we shall share. With my queen at my side, we will rebuild this kingdom from the ruins my father left it in. Together. With spinning wheels, waterwheels, and my best men scouring the country for the villain who killed my father, for I will see justice done for such a heinous crime."

"Call the guard captain. You will need his help in this. And…together, maybe you can take the body out of here." She eyed the statue of the late king and shivered. "The king would have killed me, if he had laid hands on me. When you find your father's killer, be merciful. He deserves a quick death, with as little pain as possible. For all his faults, he saved me from your father's wrath four times."

Lubos seized her hands and kissed them. "It shall be as my queen commands. My father might have lived for many years longer, letting his madness ruin the kingdom completely. Von Rumpelstiltskin has done us a great service, taking matters into his own hands. Fate has the strangest ways of making things turn out well. Now, rest, for I have much to do, including planning our coronation in the cathedral. I will be the happiest man in the world when I place my mother's crown on your head."

He helped her lie back on the pillows, then rushed from the room, shouting for Schuttmann.

Forty-Five

Chase heard the horse approaching, and he headed outside to meet Abraham. He had to see for himself if the man had really stolen the crown prince's child.

Abraham slid down from his horse, then fell to his knees in the snow. His arms were empty.

"So you are not as much of a fool as I thought," Chase said. He took the horse's bridle, intending to take the animal to the stable.

Abraham seized his cloak. "I am a fool. Such a fool. The princess is his only hope.

Isaak's only hope. When I am gone, you must take the boy to her and tell her. The king is dead. And the princess…the princess…the seer was right about the boy. She cannot be wrong about the princess. She is Isaak's only hope."

Chase shook himself free. "Go inside, and warm yourself before the fire. I will see to the horse, and you should see to your son."

He took the animal inside the tiny barn that passed for a stable, and removed the saddle and bridle before brushing the mare down. No matter how hard Abraham tried to hide his ill-health, Chase knew him too well for that. Abraham was dying, and the sickness had taken his mind already. His body would be next. Thank the heavens Maja had not lived to see the man she loved go mad.

When the horse was properly cared for, Chase returned to the cottage. Abraham sat on the chair by the fire, holding out his bare hands to the flames to warm them. His fingers were perpetually blue these days.

"Oh, Maja," Chase heard Abraham say.

Chase turned away, giving Abraham the

privacy to mourn.

Isaak's wet nurse, Ida, slept in the loft above, but Isaak's cradle was here where it was warm. The boy was the very image of his brother Heber's children, even sucking his thumb like Aran, the eldest, had. "Come and see, Abraham. Doesn't he look like Aran?" Chase asked, beckoning.

But Abraham did not answer.

Chase turned to see what had distracted his brother in law, only to find his chair was empty. A pair of dark shoes lay on the floor, full of gold coins that spilled out in a puddle on the flagstones. A pile of coins sat on the chair, too, topped by a pair of familiar golden brown, fur lined gloves. Of Abraham, there was no sign.

Forty-Six

"Your Majesties, we've found him," Captain Schuttmann announced. He lowered his voice so only the king and queen could hear. "And he had a child with him."

Molina half rose from her throne, before Lubos' hand on her shoulder gently pushed her back into her seat. She shot a glance at the packed court – would she ever get used to having an audience for everything she did? – and made a show of adjusting the cushions beneath her before planting her bottom firmly on them.

Most of the court knew nothing of Tessarina, or her pregnancy, and if anyone did, they'd probably heard the same story that circulated among the castle servants: she'd lost the baby. So if the queen wept, the servants knew the reason for her grief, or at least they thought they did.

Two guards marched a man between them, dropping him to his knees before the dais. Another guard came forward with a peasant woman, carrying a squirming bundle in her arms. The child's wet nurse, Molina guessed. Could it be Tessarina? She hardly dared hope, and yet...

"You won't find him." The kneeling man's voice was harsh as he gazed unflinchingly at Lubos, though he knew better than to rise with two guards standing over him.

Molina's breath hissed out of her. She did not know this man. They hadn't caught him after all, and the child could not be her daughter. The witch still had her.

"Find who?" Lubos asked.

"Sir Abraham von Rumpelstiltskin, the man who put down your father like the mad dog he was." The man glared. "Your Majesty," he spat, as though the title was an insult. Perhaps it was to him.

"Where is he?" Molina asked.

The man's pale eyes turned to her in surprise.

When he did not answer, Lubos said, "Your queen asked you a question, and you will answer it. Where is von Rumpelstiltskin?"

"I do not know. Out of your reach, far beyond your borders."

Lubos nodded. "Then who are you? His squire? His servant?"

The man spat on the floor. "I am Sir Chase of…of nowhere now. I left my lord's service to escort my sister to her new home, where I thought she would be safe. Alas, Maja is dead, and my former brother in law decided to commit regicide, and catch some of the old king's madness, it would seem."

"And what of the child?" Lubos asked.

"The boy is Maja's child by Abraham, her husband. Before the madness took him, he swore to give his life for the boy, for he would let no harm come to him. The last thing he asked me to do was to ensure the boy was cared for, to take him to the princess." He jerked his head toward Molina. "That would be you, I guess. If he ever regains his senses, I am certain he will come for the boy, if only to check that I kept my word."

Lubos met the man's eyes, and it seemed to Molina that he gave the tiniest of nods. He raised his voice. "The child will be placed in the royal nursery, and raised as a ward of the crown. If he shows promise he will be allowed to become a page, then a squire, and perhaps even a knight, like his father. I will keep his lands in trust for when he comes of age to be one of my loyal barons." For as a hostage in this household, he would have no choice. "Does the child have a name?"

"Maja called him Isaak," Sir Chase said. "I believe she would thank you for your kindness, Your Majesty, if she could."

"If you swear fealty, I may allow you to take him as your squire when he is of an age to do so," Lubos said.

His tone was careful, calculating, with no emotion in it at all. The tone of a monarch,

Molina realised with a shiver.

Sir Chase smiled faintly. "I thank you for the offer, Your Majesty, but we both know that is not a good idea. If Abraham were to return for the boy…ah, tell him I am far away, serving some foreign lord or court. It shall be the truth." He pulled a pair of gloves out of his pocket and threw them down on the steps. "He wanted the boy to have these. The queen will know when the time is right, I think."

Molina recoiled. She knew those gloves well, for von Rumpelstiltskin had worn them, only taking them off when he wanted to touch something to turn it to gold. Yet she nodded curtly, and gestured for a servant to pick them up and bring them to her. She didn't want to touch them. "Bring the child to the nursery. I shall…inspect him there." She beckoned to the guard with the wet nurse, as she rose from the dais and made her way out of the throne room.

Lubos found her in the nursery later that evening, watching the boy sleep. They were alone, for she'd sent the wet nurse down to the kitchen for dinner.

"Did I make the right decision?" Lubos

asked. "Or did I mess up?"

Molina smiled. In court, he was every bit the king his father had trained him to be, but in private he was the same man she'd met by the millponds. "I don't know. I don't want to ever see him again, and if we have his son, I imagine we will. Yet the boy has no one, and if he grows up, he will inherit what I understand are prosperous lands. It makes sense to raise him under your roof, so that he will see you as more of a father than the man who deserted him. And there is the matter of the princess Sir Chase spoke of. Von Rumpelstiltskin could not have meant me, for he knew I could not break his curse. Perhaps he believed Tessarina could. If his father never returns and the boy becomes a knight, you can send him out to find her."

Lubos hung his head. "I sent guards back to the witch's cottage, but they found nothing and no one. Not even the garden I saw. As if somehow…magically…it all vanished. The walls were broken ruins, yet I remember climbing them. If I had known the witch would take our daughter and disappear, I would have…"

"You would have done exactly what you have done. You have not lied to me yet, and you will not do so today. You pledged her to save my life and hers, just as I did. We are both equally culpable in this, and will suffer for it, as we deserve. Perhaps, one day, there will be other children."

Lubos blinked. "Other children? You mean…but the midwife said…"

"To wait until I am ready," Molina finished for him. "It has been some weeks since she was born. I believe tonight I might be ready to take you into my bed, so that you can fondle these before they return to their normal size." She cupped her breasts through her dress.

"Will the boy be all right alone here?" Lubos asked, casting a longing look at Molina.

She shrugged. "I have never cared for a child before, so I have no idea. The wet nurse will return soon, and he's asleep now. If his lungs are as strong as Tessarina's, he will soon wail loud enough to let someone know if he wants something."

"Then let us go to bed, and see if I can give

you an heir by morning," Lubos said eagerly, taking her arm.

"Or tomorrow night, or the night after," Molina said.

"Or any night after, for I swear I will make you happy again, Molina, happy ever after."

And she smiled, because she knew he spoke the truth.

Forty-Seven

Chase sold Abraham's horse for a good price, and tucked the coins into the pouch at his waist. He had enough money to get him to almost any kingdom in the civilised world, and for the first time in his life, he was free to choose who he served.

King Erik's court in Aros was famed for its tourneys, and he could win any archery contest with his eyes closed. Perhaps it was time to aim high and attach himself to a royal court, to see how his fortunes fared there. Better than his brother's fortune, he'd wager, for Heber's land was not so fruitful of late, or so his last letter had said.

Yes, he would go to Aros.

There was nothing left for him here. His beloved sister was dead, and his brother in arms was gone. Time he was gone, too.

Sir Chase mounted his mare, and set off on his quest for fame and fortune.

About the Author

Demelza Carlton has always loved the ocean, but on her first snorkelling trip she found she was afraid of fish.

She has since swum with sea lions, sharks and sea cucumbers and stood on spray drenched cliffs over a seething sea as a seven-metre cyclonic swell surged in, shattering a shipwreck below.

Demelza now lives in Perth, Western Australia, the shark attack capital of the world.

The *Ocean's Gift* series was her first foray into fiction, followed by her suspense thriller *Nightmares* trilogy. She swears the *Mel Goes to Hell* series ambushed her on a crowded train and wouldn't leave her alone.

Want to know more? You can follow Demelza on Facebook, Twitter, YouTube or her website, Demelza Carlton's Place at:

www.demelzacarlton.com

Books by Demelza Carlton

Siren of Secrets series
Ocean's Secret (#1)
Ocean's Gift (#2)
Ocean's Infiltrator (#3)

Siren of War series
Ocean's Justice (#1)
Ocean's Widow (#2)
Ocean's Bride (#3)
Ocean's Rise (#4)
Ocean's War (#5)
How To Catch Crabs

Nightmares Trilogy
Nightmares of Caitlin Lockyer (#1)
Necessary Evil of Nathan Miller (#2)
Afterlife of Alana Miller (#3)

Mel Goes to Hell series
Welcome to Hell (#1)
See You in Hell (#2)
Mel Goes to Hell (#3)
To Hell and Back (#4)
The Holiday From Hell (#5)
All Hell Breaks Loose (#6)

Romance Island Resort series

Maid for the Rock Star (#1)
The Rock Star's Email Order Bride (#2)
The Rock Star's Virginity (#3)
The Rock Star and the Billionaire (#4)
The Rock Star Wants A Wife (#5)
The Rock Star's Wedding (#6)
Maid for the South Pole (#7)
Jailbird Bride (#8)

Romance a Medieval Fairytale series

Enchant: Beauty and the Beast Retold
Dance: Cinderella Retold
Fly: Goose Girl Retold
Revel: Twelve Dancing Princesses Retold
Silence: Little Mermaid Retold
Awaken: Sleeping Beauty Retold
Embellish: Brave Little Tailor Retold
Appease: Princess and the Pea Retold
Blow: Three Little Pigs Retold
Return: Hansel and Gretel Retold
Wish: Aladdin Retold
Melt: Snow Queen Retold
Spin: Rumpelstiltskin Retold
Kiss: Frog Prince Retold
Hunt: Red Riding Hood Retold
Reflect: Snow White Retold
Roar: Goldilocks Retold
Cobble: Elves and the Shoemaker Retold

www.ingramcontent.com/pod-product-compliance
Lightning Source LLC
Chambersburg PA
CBHW070610170726
48291CB00003B/766